JAMMED

UP

a Debt Goes Bad novella

STEVEN HAYWARD

ACKNOWLEDGEMENTS

Writing Jammed Up has been a real joy from start to finish and I've had amazing support from a whole host of people. Firstly, I'll be forever grateful to Annabel Andrews who, with a little help from her sister Roxanne, helped bring Jam and Jabba to life through her wonderful insights into the Croydon rudeboy sub-culture and dialect. Any weaknesses in terms of authenticity — for the sake of the story or through erroneous interpretation — are entirely mine.

The incredibly honest, practical and pertinent feedback from my Beta Readers helped in the development of some crucial nuances that I hope help to make this story a worthy prequel to Mickey Take. My sincere thanks go to Linda Hughes, Jacqueline Andrews, Dominic Canty, Ed Matsumoto and Monica Carter. You are all Alphas in my eyes!

My editor Leila Dewji's creative insights, from the big-picture structural elements to the minutiae of prose and grammar, proved invaluable once again in elevating a manuscript into a novel I can be proud of.

I'm also hugely grateful to Shell Baker and the Crime Book Club; Tracy Fenton, Helen Boyce and THE Book Club; and Deryl Easton and the NotRights (all on Facebook) for a great deal of support helping to raise awareness of my writing in recent months.

Last but equally first, I'd like to thank my wife, Helen, who continues to support me on my literary journey, allowing me to keep faith in where it might one day lead.

For my dear friend Dave

Frederick David Sopp

1949 – 2014

Always look on the bright side

PROLOGUE

January 2000
Sunday

Clearing a circle in the glass with the heel of his hand, Herb Long peered out at the car-lined street. It was still and silent; too early for the usual stream of cars that even at the weekend, and on this of all days, would use it as a rat-run to the station on George Lane.

He'd bought the house a few years before, when things had been looking up. He'd needed more rooms. Apart from that, he wanted a place north of the river. After all, London was such a big city. His particular line of trade was booming and the opportunities up here were huge. And besides, whoever built a global empire in a place named after the interment of plague victims? He'd needed to branch out, but above all else, this was going to be a stepping stone that one day would allow him to retire further out in the Essex countryside. Somewhere he could feel closer to her.

Outside, it was drizzly and numbingly cold. He shuddered as he let the heavy, tattered curtain fall across the grimy window. It had been a long night and the dull shadow of a headache pulled on the muscles at the base of his skull. Rubbing his forehead, he turned and walked across the room. Yesterday, it had been stacked, floor to ceiling, with boxes, crates and cases, and its roughly-papered walls had been lined with rails of clothing. As he pulled the handle behind him, a single wire hanger lost its grip on the top of the door and bounced quietly on the dusty floorboards.

He crossed the hallway to another empty room and closed

its door firmly. Returning to the front door, he had one last thing to do before he could finally leave this place.

It was on the windowsill adjacent to the front door where he'd left it the day before. He picked up the small, glittery box and held it carefully, the lines on his face showed a mix of contempt and remorse, neither of which he could completely fathom. He shook the thoughts from his head and turned back towards the rear of the house. The small kitchen at the back was old and basic, functional but filthy, and largely unused. Apart from a table and two chairs, there was no other sign of domesticity; all its surfaces were bereft of utensils and the cupboards were empty, save for one drawer, forgotten in the dresser behind the door.

He pulled it open and a wistful smile briefly coloured his stony features. As gently as he put down the object he'd carried in, he lifted the photograph of his wife from the drawer. Her death 16 years before had been the start of all of this. Unknown to him, the man he blamed was intent on taking everything else he had.

'Jasmine,' he whispered, and his smile slowly transformed into a sorrowful frown. When a tear broke free of his lashes, he wiped it away self-consciously, looking around, embarrassed. As if in judgement, a shrill sound rang out and he reached into his pocket for the phone.

'Boss?' said an urgent Caledonian voice, gruff and familiar.

'Yeah, what?'

'Filth… here!'

'Where?'

'Greave-send.'

'What about them?' It wasn't usually this difficult to understand the big man's monosyllabic grunts.

'Oot-side.'

'What d'you mean, Mac?'

'Trying tee get in.'

'Shit! You need to get out.'

'The stuff…'

'Leave it, leave it all.'

'But Herb... what aboot...'

'We sorted it... you sorted it,' he said, and the grip of his large hand around the phone tightened as his mind went back to that night, 12 years before. The night he'd helped a young friend, spattered with blood, blubbering and inconsolable; the body of another youth lifeless on the floor. The memory of a face pierced near the eye with a sliver of wood. Of initial confusion, that such a wound could have brought him down. More so, that it could have caused so much claret. Then, he'd seen the knife.

'Aye,' came the subdued reply, but he didn't hear it. Only when the plastic phone casing reached its limit with an audible *crack*, was he pulled back into the present.

'We'll be fine,' he said, benefiting as much from the reassurance he was trying to project through the calmness of his words. When he heard shouting in the background down the line, he raised his voice: 'Get the hell out of there.'

Hitting the phone's red button, he scowled at its now-split screen and returned it inside his suit jacket. He then dropped the framed photograph he still held in his other hand into the large outer pocket of his cashmere coat. He grabbed the shimmering plastic box roughly, sending it crashing into the back of the drawer, before slamming it shut.

Through the small window to the rear, the rampant garden was barely visible in the tentative light. The Luton van had left from behind the wooden fence and the merchandise was on its way to one of his least-favoured distributors. He cursed at the thought of the low price he'd been forced to accept when already the plans to consolidate his operations were unravelling. It was too late now to call it back; his counterfeit brands business could afford to lose a slice of margin from time to time, but, more importantly, he would never take a hit on his integrity. Maybe this wouldn't be the last he'd be seeing of this godforsaken house after all. He turned and walked back across the rough floor of the large connecting room, and through the dank passageway to the front door.

3

He buttoned his coat, pulled the silk scarf up around his neck, and retrieved a hat from the banister post. Pausing momentarily to position the tan fedora and check his appearance in the door-glass, his eye was drawn down to the mat where a tiny silver numeral had caught the light. He knelt and picked it up, frowning at the shiny, plastic 2000 he held in his hand, before realising he'd probably brought the piece of confetti in yesterday on the bottom of his shoe. He crushed it between his finger and thumb and returned his attention to the more immediate problem; discovering where the weakness was in his business structure that had left it vulnerable to this latest attack.

Before he left the house to walk briskly and unseen to the Mercedes saloon parked discreetly in a neighbouring street and drive back south, the question lay heavy on his mind. Who else could have even known about that safe house? Apart from Mac, his trusted lieutenant, who, by then, had evaded the police raid and disappeared unnoticed into the dreary Gravesend dawn, there were only two other people, to his knowledge, who had been in there since he started using it for storage in '85. One of them, he hadn't seen for several years, but he couldn't entertain the possibility that the lad might be involved in this breach. As for the other one, he was long-since dead and buried.

1.

Fifteen Months Later
Tuesday

The question came from beneath the aluminium bench, where his boss of two days was drilling holes through a bracket into the cinderblock wall.

'Kick that chuck key over, Kingston, will you?'

"S'Jam,' he said, dropping his arms gratefully from where they had been reaching up to screw the heavy gauge hinge to the metal frame. The reinforced door he was fitting wasn't yet secure and he held it steady as he kicked the key across the rough concrete floor.

'Oh yeah, sorry,' the boss said, as he took it up and started unlocking the drill bit. 'What kind of a street name is that, anyway?'

"S'ma tag,' Jam said, getting a frown in return. 'Graffin', yeah.'

'Oh, I get it.' The boss rolled his eyes. 'So, you're saying if I see the word Jam plastered all over the side of a train, that was your handiwork?'

'I was jus' a youngsta.'

'Vandalism, that's what I call it.'

'Nah, man.' Jam shook his head, feeling misunderstood. 'But I don't do dat no more.'

'And why Jam?'

'Dunno. Cos I like jam, innit.'

'You're called Jam because you like *jam*?'

'Not now, man. When I was likkle, yeah. Dat's da only fing I'd eat.'

'I thought it was short for Jamaica but you said you're from down south; Croydon, wasn't it?'

'Yer get me. Ma mum still live dere, Fornton Heaf, yeah.'

'And Dad?'

'Dunno. Never met him.'

'Bastard.'

'Wha'jer mean?'

'No, not you. I meant...'

Jam relaxed his jaw. 'Joker.'

'I bet you had to put up with a lot of stick having a nickname like that... when you were a kid?' He disappeared back under the ledge and began drilling again.

'Me?' Jam shouted above the noise. 'Nah, man. No one start on me. I was boxin' at eight. Knockin' out teenagers at ten. No one call me names.'

'Boxing? Back in Croydon?' The drilling stopped and the boss turned to look at him.

'When I was a kid, yeah, I'm on ma way home from da shop. I was big for ma age an' dese yoot, not from our ends, jump me. I fought back. I can't go home wivout ma muvver's food, but dey bang me up.'

'You sound like a brave little kid. I would never have done that.' The boss took up the drill again and returned to his task.

'Nah, man,' Jam said, shaking his head. 'Jus' when I fink I'm goin' to get home wiv ma Mum's shoppin' yeah, dey jack it an' beat me some more.'

'Bloody *'ell*.'

'After dat, ma uncle get me in da gym an' learn me to box. No one ever do dat to me again.'

'So you were never Jam Tart then? Or Jammy Dodger?' The boss allowed himself a grin, intent on lifting the mood while putting his new trainee back in his place. 'Or maybe when you were older... I bet they called you Jam Rag?'

The young man scoffed. 'Clown. Nah, man. Remember ma bredrin', Karl Brown an' Matt Lamont?'

'Who?'

'Double Trouble... Street Tuff... Come on cuz, you gotta keep up. Kiss FM, yeah?'

'I've no idea...'

'Tuff Enough Brown...? Jam Lamont...? Bes DJs on da radio, man.'

'Really? And...?'

'Dey call Tuff Jam,' he sang out with a swagger. 'Dat's me, Tuff Jam.'

'Yeah, right,' the guvnor said, and banged his head on the metal ledge as he lowered himself back under. 'If you're so *Tough Jam*, why haven't you got that bloody door on yet?'

'I'm gettin' dere. Anyway man, dey're proper heavy. Why you need metal doors in a grimy place like dis?'

'Oi, watch your lip. And keep your opinions to yourself if you want to come back again tomorrow. We just do what we're told and we get paid. Got it?'

'You're da boss.'

'That's right. Just keep your head down.' He slid back under the wide metal shelf to resume drilling, and over the din yelled, 'And I want that other door fitted before you slope off today.'

At a nearby café, later that afternoon, Jam was on the phone to his best friend.

Jabba was white, but they shared the same street dialect. Grounded in the youth subculture of Lonjam, theirs was an intimidating mongrel of South London and Jamaican parentage; a patois, rich with biting satire and linguistic inventiveness that continuously evolved. Several years of living north of the river had dulled their edge and back home, they would now have been considered outsiders. But whenever the young men came together, they reverted to the Croydon Rudeboy personas of their teenage years.

'It was mental, bruv,' Jam said. 'I'm meant to keep it on da d-low. Dat place is proper bait.'

'Wh'appen, bruv?' Although a couple of years older, Jabba spoke with the eager curiosity of a child, symptomatic of the mild cerebral palsy he'd suffered at birth. Their friendship was such that Jam no longer noticed.

'Oh my days, blood,' Jam said, 'It's a big-arse grimy house, all mash up wiv two room from breeze block.'

'An extension?'

'Nah, man. Inside da house, innit. Da windows all bruck up. Concrete floor. An' *bare* likkle rooms. An' I'm puttin' in dese doors, yeah. Metal. Proper big.'

'Dat's deep. Like a jail?'

'Yer get me, or a safe.'

'Jokes.' Jam's friend laughed. 'Safes don't have doors like dat, bruv.'

'Yeah, dey do. Wha'bout bank vaults?'

'Oh yeah, like in dat film...'

'For real. So today, dis guy turn up. He's *big* boy, like dat bouncer at Blue Orchid down south, remember... but a sporran, yeah, like Bre'vart wivout da blue face, man.' Jam's friend sniggered. 'He's frontin' da boss, yeah, cos da locks ain't on da doors yet. I'm finkin' I'm gonn'ave to step in.'

'Wha'jer do, Jam?'

'I tell da boss-boss to chill an' we'll get dem all fitted before we leave, but Bre'vart's like *"No gud enough"* an' den he grab ma boss by his top an' say he need to lock sumfink away now.'

'Oh ma gosh!'

'Ma boss is proper vexed boy an' he goes well pale, yeah, an' I'm finkin he's a old man, he's at lease forty, he's gonna get a heart attack. Lau it man! Someone gonna get bus' up.'

'Innit dough.'

'I say why you need a house like dis for? An' when Breve-boy just grunt, I arks him, you gonna lock Uncle Fester in one of dem rooms?'

'Dat's jokes. Like Da Addams Family.'

'Den he goes all Tyson on ma arse an' says *"Fock ye"*. An' he looses ma boss an' when I tell him to go fuck *himself*, he tries to clutch *me*. So I step in man.'

'Lau *dat!*' His friend's voice was now deadly serious.

'Uh-uh, you know. I spark him an' he drop.'

'Rude*boy!*'

'But den dis uvver new guy come in. Old, old wiv grey hair an' ev'ryfink...'

'Nah, Uncle Fester bald, man.'

'Yeah, haha, but no, dis guy tough, like Tommy Lee Jones wiv a buzz cut. He tell me to stop an' den ma boss is dere behind him screamin' at me as well.'

'Liber'ies!'

'Yeah man an' now it's like I'm da one dat's wrong, yeah, an' Bre'vart's still on da floor, yeah, squirmin' and holdin' hi'self where I tump him in da stomach. I'm *screwin'* bruv. Den all of us step back an' look at each uvver wond'rin' wh'appen.'

'You lose your job, bruv?'

'Nah... but... yeah. Ma boss say piss off an' don't come back.'

'Uh-uh, you know.'

'Yer get me. Anyway, before I can even get ma hoodie, yeah bruv, da old-old guy yank me into da front room, an' I'm finkin' – What now? But he all calm an' compose an' he say sit down but I don't. And den I do, yeah, cos I fink dis might be interestin'. An' he say I shouldna hit dat big guy an' I should say sorry to him. But Jam ain't apologisin' for *nuffink,* boy.'

'You *know* dat.'

'Den he say he got a idea, maybe some way I can make fings all betta. He'll still pay me to da end of da week, yeah, if I go see him on Friday. Won't promise nuffink but he might give me some uvver work, yeah. An' I'm finkin', safe, yeah.'

'Heavy!'

'Yeah, movin' stuff from uvver places into dis one. He's got bare houses in Souf London but one of dem had to be abandon, an dey had to change dis one up so dey can start usin' it again, yeah. He finks if I help out by workin' wiv da big guy we might make up our difference. I tell him dat big guy don't scare me but he shake his head like da man is all dat, and he say I have to be careful.'

'Oh ma days. Down south? Down our ends?'

'But not, innit. It's far. Greenhithe. Some place like dat.'

'Is dat near Croydon?'

'Nah bruv. Nowhere near... You can come if you like.'

'Nah fanks, bruv,' said Jabba, 'I'll stay in ma own yard.'

***

Although North Kent's youngest ever Area Commander rarely turned from his desk to contemplate the irony, the window of his third floor Gravesend office presented an unrestricted panorama of Northfleet Cemetery.

'Do we know whose property it is yet, Inspector?' He was thumbing through a report and continued without looking up.

'We're still not entirely sure, sir.' The recently-promoted detective inspector stopped gazing at the view over his new boss's shoulder and stared instead at the top of his prematurely-balding head. For several weeks, he had studied his superior's demeanour for some small sign of camaraderie on which to bridge the apparent gulf between them. Sitting in front of him now, the DI could scarcely believe the rumours that the AC was not yet thirty-five and his hand went involuntarily to rake the thick pile of his own hair. 'The tip-off said local organised crime-lord, but we've come to a complete dead end on that one.'

'So, by *not entirely sure*,' the senior officer looked up momentarily, 'you mean, no.'

'Sir.'

'But someone had to have bought the house. Surely, there must be conveyance records, payment details, bank accounts... something.'

'Yes, sir, Financial Investigations have been all over it. Got as far as a German-sounding name... Anglich.' He pointed at the file. 'It's all in there.'

'And where are we with Herr Anglich?'

'Er... as the report says... sir. Likely to be a fake identity.'

'So, what about all the gear, any trace on the origin?'

'Some of it's legit, just not authenticated, so to speak, by the brand owners. Like it just dropped out of the supply chain. The rest of it, replicas, mostly from China. All very high quality. Some of the companies couldn't even be certain whether it was really theirs or not. It's all been photographed and catalogued, but nobody's likely to come forward to claim any of it.'

'What did the local neighbours tell us?'

'Very little... sir.'

'What do you mean?' The frown in the AC's forehead seemed to bring his receding hairline forward by an inch.

'Well... no one seemed to know anything. No one remembered seeing anything suspicious. Nothing out of the ordinary.'

'Nothing... out of the ordinary?'

'That's right, sir.'

'Let me get this clear, Inspector. We discovered half a million pounds' worth of unregistered and counterfeit luxury goods sitting in a small residential house on a quiet street in the middle of Gravesend, and no one saw anything... out of the ordinary?'

'Sir.'

'Christ! Anyone would think we were dealing with a few tinny Rolexes knocked out the back of a yellow three-wheeler in Peckham High Street, Inspector. What is the matter with people? Don't they realise this is the life-blood of serious organised crime?'

The detective inspector acknowledged the unexpected humour with a sardonic smile. 'More interested in saving a few quid, sir,' he countered, 'so they can impress their mates down the pub.'

'Well they won't be so bloody blasé when their kids are all crack-heads and their BMWs and flat-screen TVs keep getting nicked to feed the vicious circle.'

'Indeed, sir. The myth of the victimless crime.'

'Idiots.'

'Yes, sir.'

'What about physical evidence?'

'Forensics worked on it for months, sir. There was so much stuff in there. But no leads. Nothing. Everything was clean.'

'Well that's certainly ironic.'

'Yes, sir.'

'Where is it all now?'

'Awaiting destruction, sir. Just needs your authorisation. There, at the front.' He pointed again.

'Okay, Inspector.' The AC closed the file and began tracing his finger down the pro-forma clipped to the front. 'I can't say I'm entirely happy about it. But if this is your recommendation...'

'Sir, if I can be blunt...' He waited briefly for a reaction but his boss continued reading. 'We just don't have the resource or the budget to go around chasing ghosts... sir.'

'Well, I'll be the first to agree with you there, Inspector...' The AC looked up, exhaling deeply, and reached for his pen. 'I'll sign this, only because I want this case closed. If disposing of all this... contraband brings that day closer, so much the better. And I want your team back doing some proper police work. Ticking off more of the things at the top of the Chief Constable's list of priorities.'

'You and me both, sir.'

'And what about the house?'

'That's a different story, sir. Hoping for legal seizure. But we'll need to convince a judge it's the proceeds of crime.'

'Hmm. And I suppose without a criminal to connect it to, that's going to be a can of worms.'

'Yes, sir.'

'Keep me informed, Inspector.'

'I will sir... Oh, and sir? There was one other thing.'

'Go on.'

'The blood stain... beneath the floorboards.'

'I thought that line of enquiry was already closed.'

'It was sir, pending formalities. And Forensics have now finalised their report.'

'It says... in here, Inspector,' he raised the report off the desk with both hands, 'they've already confirmed with the

12

amount of bleaching compound used, the sample was too old and too degraded for a reliable DNA match. Suggests we've just been waiting for them to get off the fence and put that in writing. Fair assessment?'

'Yes, sir… but with their report now in… it's right at the back there… apart from not ruling out the possibility the retained samples might one day offer potential matches…'

'Of course,' the AC cut in. 'We're seeing advances all the time in the profiling technology.'

'Quite, sir. But they've also added there's some degree of certainty there would have been a lot more blood under the floor than previously thought.'

'Go on.'

'Well, either someone slowly and completely bled out, which they say is unlikely because the heart usually stops pumping long before that…'

'Or?'

'It was sufficient quantity to have been… multiple deaths.'

'Jesus!'

'I think they may have been exaggerating, sir… when they said to me off the record, it's the sort of quantity you'd expect to find in an abattoir.'

'Oh, great! Now what am I going to tell the Chief Super?'

***

After ending the call to his friend, Jam looked up to find that all the other customers had now left the café and the girl who'd served him with the all-day breakfast was clearing the vacated tables. He mopped up the egg yolk with the crust of his bread and repeatedly glanced across at her to see if she would look back. He didn't want much from life, but one of his daily goals was to secure the smile of a pretty girl and all day long, he'd been stuck in that grimy, old house fitting doors and shelves.

She busied herself loading the plates onto a tray and then wiped the table clean. When she turned to head back to the

13

kitchen, she peered across to the only occupied table, and smiled when the young man returned her gaze.

He waited for her to reappear but when some guy acting like he owned the place came for his plate, he dropped the exact money for his food in small change onto the table and left. He was in no hurry to go home to the damp room in the upstairs flat that his ageing auntie rented in Mile End. And anyway, it was still rush-hour and all those bankers needed to get home for their tea. He felt a bit like a stalker, waiting along the street from the café, hoping there wasn't a rear exit by which she might have already left. He only wanted to get another smile. And maybe ask her name.

He watched as a tube train arrived at the platform at South Woodford, and moments later, a stream of people exited the station and crossed the road towards him. He didn't know the area at all before yesterday, but it felt like a nice enough place. He stepped back from the kerb to let people pass and took the packet of Marlboro from his coat pocket. Then he remembered tossing his dead lighter into someone's dustbin when he walked away from the house earlier.

'Scuse me, cuz. You gotta li...' The man in the suit walked past without the slightest reaction; he could have been in a parallel universe. Jam slumped back against the wall.

'Scuse me, lady.' That time, there was at least some acknowledgement he existed, but the woman shook her head without waiting for the question and strode past him into a shop.

'Did you want a light?' It was a young female voice and he spun around, gratefully. Standing in front of him, holding up a lit cigarette, was the waitress from the café.

'Fank you,' he said, putting his own cigarette to his lips and leaning in to take the light from hers. 'Startin' to fink I'm invisible or sumfink.'

'Wrong time of day to expect any humanity around here,' she said, looking about her at the frustrated faces, silently blustering at the obstruction she was causing in the middle of the pavement.

14

'Fanks,' he said. 'Glad I ain't beggin' fa food. Man could starve.'

'What? After all you've just eaten?'

'Ay, best meal of da day, dat.'

'Yeah, when you eat it in the morning!' That time when she smiled, he almost fell into her eyes.

'What way you goin'?' He stepped forward to look in the direction she was heading, oblivious to the three people who had to break their stride to walk around him. 'I jus' waitin', you know, for da trains to lighten up. Rough to be lock up wiv dis lot.'

'I don't blame you...' she said. 'Me? I haven't got far to go. Bit of a walk, but I prefer to stretch my legs after standing all day.'

At that moment, he couldn't stop himself from looking down. She was wearing sturdy flats. Sensible shoes, his auntie would have called them. Yet, even through her heavy black tights, he could see the outline of a shapely calf tapering to a slender ankle.

'Nice,' was the only word that came out, and when he looked back at her face, she was staring at him quizzically.

'Anyway,' she said, 'nice to meet you. Enjoy your cigarette.'

'Yeah, fanks... you too.'

'Bye then.'

'Ah... I could walk wiv you, you know.'

'It's okay, I know the way.' She smiled. 'And you'd be getting too far from the station.'

'But... I owe you... for da light. Wha'bout a drink? Dere's a pub jus' round da corner.'

'Look, I really need to get home.' Her voice was firmer as she stepped to the side.

'Okay,' he said, shrugging his shoulders. 'At lease tell me your name.'

'Maybe next time,' she said, before heartlessly dousing his satisfied smile by adding, 'I'm already late for the childminder.'

'Ah... okay.' His face dropped. 'Right den. Okay, I'll see you in da caf again, yeah.'

15

'Yeah, you do that.' She nodded. 'I'll see you next time.'

'You proper will, baby,' he said, as he watched her sculpted calves walk away.

By the time she reached the end of the street, she had blended into the flow. Jam decided to spend the evening in the gym and avoid explaining the latest twist in his working arrangements to his reluctant landlady. He crossed the road towards the station without seeing the young waitress look around and smile before she turned right and continued walking down the side-street towards home.

***

Meanwhile, from a Northfleet public phone box:

'George, it's Terry Pinner. About that gear.'

'Yes, Tel?'

'Just had the green light. Secure disposal at the Chatham depot, tomorrow. Usual sub-contractors departing Gravesend. Tell Ray, if he still wants it, it's ten per cent to the driver and—'

'And what?'

Pinner swallowed hard. 'Tell your boss that as far as I'm concerned, this makes me and him even. He'll understand.'

'I dunno about that, Tel. But I reckon he'll be well 'appy. I'll give you a shout later to confirm.' George Harris paused long enough for Pinner to relax. 'Just one thing though, Tel.'

'What's that?'

'He ain't my boss, right? We're partners.'

'That's what you think,' Detective Inspector Pinner said, after replacing the handset.

On the walk back to the office, Terry Pinner reflected on the debt he could finally settle with the untouchable Raymond Riggs. He had known the man for many years, going back before his own secondment to the Royal Gibraltar Police. As teenagers, they had played amateur football together until Riggs was taken onto the books at Colchester. And then there was that tragic accident that ended a promising career. Pinner liked to think he'd just been in the right place at the right time. But there were times he'd ask himself the question: was it wrong place, wrong time?

Only after he returned to North Kent with his wife and young son from the offshore posting, did Pinner reconnect with Riggs and start helping him out with the occasional nugget of sensitive information, in exchange for hard cash and luxury holidays. But nothing he could do seemed to ease his wife's growing sense of loss from her miscarriage and her resulting inability to conceive a sibling for Simon. Always one for big gestures, Riggs one day proposed a ludicrous solution that Pinner not only failed to take seriously, but failed to dismiss unequivocally. Unknown to him, wheels were then set in motion that he became powerless to stop.

Back then, he couldn't begin to contemplate how costly the outcome would be. After the adoption went through unchallenged, expectations remained that Pinner was still on the team, but the envelopes of fifty-pound notes no longer arrived and the family of four had to settle for package trips to the Costa del Sol. For five years, he'd continued to put his career at risk with no further reward and only a vague sense of the ill-defined debt slowly receding.

Even when this huge opportunity had fallen into his lap a year before, the risk seemed too great, and Pinner had kept the idea to himself. His instincts to pursue an anonymous tip-off had led to the raid on the house in Gravesend, the discovery of a treasure trove of illegal goods and, ultimately to his own promotion.

Several weeks later, he'd been summoned to a rare audience with Riggs. Under pressure to deliver something meaningful to retain the arrogant old sod's confidence, he had brazenly, perhaps foolishly, advocated his audacious proposition. To Pinner's surprise and continuing anxiety, Riggs had been thrilled, as much by the copper's bravado as by the windfall such a simple heist could generate.

Riggs, perhaps doubtful that such a plan could succeed, had

inferred that a positive outcome would equate to a balancing credit in Pinner's overdrawn account. But patience wasn't Riggs' strong suit and the weight of expectation on Pinner was becoming unbearable. Now, as Pinner strode confidently back towards the building, he sensed the burden finally lifting and allowed himself to think about how his lifestyle might benefit again from a tax-free supplementary income.

***

When the call interrupted the game of Snake he was playing on his phone, Jam had just surfaced from the tube station, less than two minutes' walk from his auntie's flat.

'Yeah, man?'

'We spoke earlier... in South Woodford. After your disagreement with one of my... associates.'

'Oh, right. Yeah. You're da old... older guy. You want me to come see you Friday.'

'That's right. That's what I'm calling about.'

'You didn't give me no address.'

'There's been a change of plan. I need you to check something out for me, tomorrow. I want you in Chatham first thing.'

'Huh? Where?'

'It's just off the A2.'

'I know dat. I got no wheels, dough.'

'Oh!' There was a long pause. 'It would have been better if you did, but it's not the end of the world.'

'Wha's in Cha'ham anyway, anuvver of dem houses?'

'No, I need you to go and check something.'

'Check what?' Jam got out his keys and quietly unlocked the front door.

'I don't want to say too much over the phone. There's a secure incineration site there and a lorry will arrive sometime after nine. I'll text you the details.'

'Okay, an'...'

18

'All you need to do is watch what happens and report back to me.'

'Nuffink else?' Jam kept his voice low as he went upstairs, stepping carefully over the ones he knew would creak.

'For now.'

'And you'll pay me till Friday?'

'As we agreed.'

'Why jer need to know wh'appen wiv da lorry?' At the top of the stairs, he slipped into his room and closed the door.

'It's what's inside I'm interested in. It belongs to me. Or at least it did.'

'You gonna try an' get it back?'

'No. It's too late for that.'

'So, it all get burned den.'

'That's why I need you there. To see that it is.'

'You want it destroyed?'

'Suffice to say, if I can no longer have it, I want to be damn sure no one else can.'

'Yeah, but why me?' Jam sat down on the narrow bed that was wedged in the corner of the room behind an old, battered wardrobe. He pulled his gym bag from underneath and went through his kit.

'You've got balls, lad. I think you're one of us; small fish swimming with sharks. Losing that stuff was a big blow, but we're getting back on our feet. I just reckon we could be very good for each other. Let's see how tomorrow goes, first.'

'Dat it?'

'That's it. Whatever happens, don't get involved, just watch. If the lorry pulls in and the doors close, that's all I need to know. But if anything else happens, I need to know that too. Just stay out of sight. Got it.'

'Let me fink about it, yeah?'

'What's there to think about? I thought you needed a job. And I need to know if you're the sort I can rely on. If you're not up to it lad, just say it now. If you'd rather spend the rest of your life doing odd jobs for a living, no skin off my nose.'

19

'Tell me again wha's in it for me?' Jam said, adding clean socks and a vest to the bag before sniffing and returning the oversized shorts that were still in there from last week.

'Trust me, lad. I keep my word. Think of this as a chance to show me you can do the same.'

'Okay... so I go dere, watch wh'appen, den what?'

'Just do the job and I'll be back in touch. And don't bother saving any of the phone numbers – you won't be able to ring or text me back. So, are you in or not?'

'Yeah man.'

'Good lad. One last thing.'

'What?'

'If you tell a living soul about this... or if you do anything stupid tomorrow, like being seen or worse still, getting caught... I'm not going to be able to guarantee your safety, understand?'

'For real,' Jam said slowly, his heart beginning to race. He'd chat it over with the punch bag first and look out for the text later. He pressed the red button on his Nokia 8210 and dropped it in his bag. Grabbing his Walkman on the way out of the room, he slipped quietly down the stairs and out the front door. He pulled up the hood on his new Nike top, and with N'n'G playing in his ears, jumped back on the tube to Bethnal Green, where he walked the rest of the way to the Boys' Club on Cheshire Street.

On the phone, later that evening:

'Jabba... 's'Jam. Come to ma yard, now yeah.'

2.

Wednesday

An articulated lorry pulled into a lay-by on the A226 just as, a few miles further south, the early sunlight washed the cold, granite walls of Rochester Castle with a golden hue.

'Won't be a minute,' the driver said, engaging the airbrake and killing the engine. He'd pulled off the road, saying he needed to answer the call of nature, but before he opened the door, he added, 'Waste of bleeding time, this trip, Phil.'

'Why? What is this lot today then, Andy?' the guy in the passenger seat said. He started feeling with his right arm behind his seat for the manifest but his seatbelt limited his reach.

'Load of old junk, I think,' Andy replied, leaning into the back of the cab to grasp the clipboard before his mate could find it. 'Waste of tax-payers' money, too, if you ask me. Why we need to go through the secure-disposal protocols for this lot, I've no idea.'

'What does it say?'

'It never tells you much, does it, mate.' He flicked over the pages without attempting to read them. 'Looks to me like a load of rubbish from some old dear's house clearance. I did hear something about it being a run-down, old place. Probably popped her clogs and all her worldly possessions were a stack of wormy furniture and a pile of rags in a wardrobe.'

'Big trailer for that though, innit?'

'Er, yeah,' Andy blustered, struggling to make light of his colleague's not unreasonable confusion, without giving away any of the details he'd been told to keep to himself. 'I heard she was one of them hoarders; piled floor to ceiling with papers and junk, never threw nothin' away.'

'So wha's all the fuss?'

'Like I said, waste of money. But...' He tapped the side of his nose with his index finger. 'Someone said she was connected to a German gangland Mr Big...'

'Oooh!' said Andy. 'Herr Grosse!'

'Ha ha! Nice one! Anyway, seems there could be some long-since stolen goods mixed up with it, and a few dodgy documents and the like.'

'And they're just gonna burn it all? Couldn't there be some useful evidence in with it? Wouldn't they wanna trace the owners?'

'You know what it's like. They don't have the manpower to sift through all this crap. It's all ancient history; probably any victims are long gone too. And if you ask me, I reckon the top brass is keen to bury it. Apparently, he just wants this lot burned and out of the way. Area Commander authorised it himself. Least... that's what I heard.'

'You don't think it's classified or anything, do you?'

'Nah, it's just old toot. And we're gonna have to hang around for hours till it's all processed. I dunno about you, Phil, but I reckon we could cut some corners with this load.'

'So, what you sayin', Andy? We've still gotta go through the procedures.'

'Yeah, course. But... look, I got an old mate who I sometimes put a bit of stuff through. You know, old records, repro furniture, the odd dodgy bitta bling. I reckon he'll drop us a monkey each to take this off our hands. What d'you think?'

'I thought you said it was all junk?'

'Yeah... to you and me. There's some these days call it vintage... prepared to pay a lot of money for genuine... old stuff. I reckon there could be a few grand here. Gotta be worth a shout.'

'Oh, I dunno, Andy. What about the paperwork?'

'Don't you worry about a bitta paperwork, mate. I know people who can sort that out.'

'What people? At the depot?'

'The site manager… owes me big time. All I have to do is put in a call.'

'That easy?'

'Yeah. You'd be surprised. There's always someone who can bend the rules for something this low-level. Trust me, Phil. It'll be fine.'

'Only 500 quid? Not sure it's worth the risk, is it?'

'Alright mate, now I've got your interest, that's just for starters. There's easy money to be made with little jobs like this. If you're in on this one, I'll remember you next time.'

'You *'ave* done this before, yeah?'

'Stop worrying, mate. I'll go and have that piss and make a quick call.' He clutched the manifest as he opened his door, and before climbing down, turned back to Phil, 'And then, I'll show you how to disable the tracker.'

***

Jam was in position. He'd found a deserted factory building with line of sight to the outer iron gates of the secure waste disposal depot. He got there before nine and now it was half ten. He'd dragged a bench over to the window and was perched on its edge but his arse cheeks were starting to complain. He put down the binoculars his mate had loaned him and rubbed his eyes. He wasn't sure he was cut out for this type of work. In the last hour, a few Transits and box-vans had come and gone, and each time he re-read the text message from the previous evening.

He'd had no idea what the word 'articulated' meant but the rest of the information was clear: red cab, most likely a silver trailer, X-reg number plate, two men on-board. The lorry should pull in through the gates and on into the inner compound, out of sight. It could be in there for several hours, but when it re-appeared, it would stop on the weigh-bridge before papers were exchanged and then be driven back through the main gates and return in the direction from which it had come. All he had to do was watch to see that it all happened without any variation.

Another hour went by and he started feeling hungry. He hadn't eaten since the all-day breakfast the previous afternoon; he rarely ate in the mornings and even if he'd wanted to, he hadn't had time today. His mind wandered from thoughts of his last meal to the waitress at the café. He started to imagine what her perfume would smell like up close. Gently brushing the side of her neck with his cheek, he could almost feel her breath against his ear, becoming deeper and uneven. Then he remembered her say she needed to relieve the child-minder and his daydream dissipated into thin air.

He poured another coffee from the flask he'd had the foresight to bring, but wished he'd made some sandwiches to go with it. Even a packet of crisps would have been something. Realisation that he could be stuck here for hours only made his stomach gripe even more. And now, come to think of it, after three cups of coffee, what would he do when he needed to pee? To distract himself, he picked up the binoculars and started scanning the inner courtyard of the depot.

Two men, who were chatting idly near the weigh-bridge, were joined by a third, who opened the paper bag he was carrying and proceeded to offer out what looked like bacon rolls. The discussion ended while the three of them ate. Jam's belly growled louder while he scanned right towards the outer gates. A man standing in a booth at the barrier was deep in conversation on a walkie-talkie and kept looking down at his papers. He nodded as he spoke and then ended the call. Jam was about to sweep away from him, when the guy started looking out of the gates towards the road. When Jam tried to pull back to see what the gateman was looking at, his view suddenly went dark.

Initially, he thought it was the window frame, and he tried panning back to where he'd been looking before, but as he refocused the magnification, he began to see an outline, and blurred but bold colours that hadn't previously been in his eye-line all the time he'd been watching. In the split second that he saw a lorry with a red cab pull through the gates beyond the object of his immediate focus, he also recognised the outline of a figure, way too close for comfort.

When he lowered the binoculars, the full horror of his situation was revealed. A thick-set man was standing outside, less than ten yards from the window. He had a heavy spanner in his hand and he was looking right into Jam's soul.

While Jam was about to get to know the wrong end of a monkey wrench, there were other eyes on the truck that rolled unchallenged into the depot. Once it had come to a stop on the weigh-bridge, the outer gates having closed behind it, the driver and the man riding shotgun stepped down from the cab. After a brief pause while the gate-keeper compared his paperwork with the clipboard held out by the driver and scanned the latter with a hand-held device, the signal was given for the inner gates to be rolled back. The two men from the lorry then walked over to a Portakabin and went inside, as a thirty-something woman in yellow overalls came out of the depot and climbed into the driver's seat. Within a minute of the lorry arriving, it was out of sight and the gate-man had returned to his booth.

Everything had happened as it should and it was now just a matter of time before the truck would re-emerge, be weighed again, and driven away by the two men, who, at that moment, were trying to keep calm in the waiting area. One pair of eyes studied the scene with resigned satisfaction before a phone was flipped open and stubby fingers tapped in a text. Elsewhere, another watcher had frozen, mid-bite of a sausage roll, and was now scanning the surrounding area with a full mouth and an increasing sense of panic.

***

Standing with Phil at the counter of the little tearoom set up at one end of the Portakabin, Andy was trying to decide between a pasty and a bacon roll. Phil had lost his appetite and only wanted a cup of tea.

'Sugar's on the table.' The cashier handed Phil his change.

'Ta luv.' He was going to need at least three spoonfuls.

'I thought you said we'd be getting home early,' he said, as Andy joined him at the table, setting down a steaming Styrofoam cup and a paper plate.

'Jesus, Phil... keep it down, mate,' Andy mouthed, looking furtively back towards the woman at the counter. Apart from her, they had the little room to themselves.

'Yeah, okay. Sorry, but...'

'Look, we still have to go through the motions, don't we?' Andy wrapped his mouth around the pasty and bit through its deceptively-cool skin, until its molten contents sizzled on the roof of his mouth.

'I know, I know... but, I was gonna say it didn't look like any house clearance I've ever seen.'

'Believe me,' Andy's words were now punctuated by tentative chewing and the puffing of his cheeks, 'I didn't know there was... *that* much stuff in there. Trouble is, we're now a lot later... than I thought we'd be... so we just need to act like everything's... normal, okay?'

'Who were those guys, anyway?' Phil said, wincing at his colleague's obvious discomfort.

'Forget about them, Phil. Trust me on this. The less you know about them, the better. Okay?'

'Okay. But why couldn't we have just unhitched the trailer and brought the other one with us?'

'Bloody 'ell, Phil. It's not that simple, is it?'

'But I thought you said your insider would just nod it through.'

'Yeah... and don't forget that jobsworth on the front gate.' Andy's voice had risen in annoyance and this time it was Phil who looked around the room. Even though the woman was now outside smoking, Andy took the hint and continued in a whisper. 'Did you see the way he was looking at the tailgate seal?'

'Yeah, I did. That's the bit I'm worried about; what happens when that woman backs it up to the incinerator and goes blabbing to the boss when she finds it's been tampered with?'

'She won't.'
'Howdya know?'
'There's only one person gets to open the back.'
'The boss.'
'Exactly.'
'Well?'
'She *is* the boss. Now drink your tea and stop worrying.'

***

Jabba had settled into his cosy hideout before watching his best friend find the perfect vantage point. The plan was for Jam to watch the depot and Jabba to watch him. It wasn't much of a plan, and when the time had come for him to do what he was there for and raise the alarm, Jabba had been too busy eating.

Unlike Jam's honed physique and strong, wiry athleticism, Jabba was below average height and morbidly obese. And unlike Jam, he'd never thrown a punch in anger. His only quality as a fighter was that he knew—all too well—how to take one. He'd never really thought about why Jam had taken him under his wing in Year 7 at Ingram High all those years before and protected him ever since. He just knew he would always be safe when his friend was nearby.

Even so, while bunnin' a zoot together in Jam's room – windows open – the previous night, Jabba had insisted he didn't want to come south of the river. It was only after Jam explained that Chatham was not only south of the Thames but also south of another river called The Medway—as well as being miles away to the east, and even more miles from their past—did he finally agree, subdued by the effects of the cannabis, to tag along.

Now, a sense of loyalty, combined with the feeling that, at long last, he might actually be able to pay his mate back for liberating him from a world of suffering as a kid, eclipsed his deep-seated instinct to run away at the first sign of trouble. Instead, he remained riveted to the spot, perched precariously as he was on the creaking frame of an old deckchair, and watched as the man wielding a lump of cold iron kicked in the door behind which he knew Jam was hiding.

He wanted to spring to his feet, push his way outside and sprint across the compound to his friend's aid... he imagined himself arriving at the splintered door, backlit like a phantom, casting a dark shadow across the floor. The thug turning around from punishing Jam, and gulping as he slowly took in the ominous threat of this new adversary, dropping the spanner with a hollow clang and running from the scene like a werewolf into the night. Then Jabba would race to his friend's side and heal his awful wounds with a single touch...

But he didn't move until he saw his friend run through the doorway with all his limbs still intact. When finally, released from his torpor, he opened the door of the garden shed and lumbered across the road towards Jam who, noticing the movement, shouted something at him.

'Jer get him, blood?' Jabba shouted back. But his words also went unheard. Now Jam was pointing and his shouting was getting frantic, but Jabba still couldn't hear what he said and kept shuffling towards him. He couldn't understand why, when he was running as fast as his bulbous frame would allow, they didn't seem to be getting any closer. Then he realised Jam was actually veering away from him now, while still turning his head in Jabba's direction, seemingly waving him away. Off to his left, the next thing to catch Jabba's eye was the man emerging from Jam's hideaway. He was moving slowly on heavy legs and now, instead of brandishing a wrench, his hands were clutching his face.

Jabba punched the air with joy, but as he did, his own feet seemed to get in the way of each other, and before he knew what was happening, he'd gone to ground in a rippling mass of grazed knees and broken wind. His chin was the last thing to hit the tarmac and once more in his troubled life, he tasted blood. He lifted his face from the ground and looked across at Jam, smiling through bloodied teeth to dismiss his clumsiness. But Jam wasn't smiling back. Even though the man behind him was beginning to speed up, Jam had stopped running and was now staring wide-eyed. In slow-motion, he was waving and Jabba tried to lift his arm to wave back...

The cut on his chin was nothing. The bitten tongue, he'd known worse. Shredded trouser legs, yeah, whatever. But whilst it was a glancing blow, the impact to the side of his head at that moment was a new experience. He couldn't be sure if it was the receding sound of Jam shouting, 'No-o-o-o!' or the sudden flow of blood in his ears, but it was the last thing he heard before his head hit the ground again.

3.

It had been another early start for Siobhan Jennings. With her dad back to working nights, there was no one to help her get the baby up, washed, nappy changed, dressed and fed, and then settled in her favourite bouncy chair before she could grab a quick shower for herself. The childminder arrived at six and she would then walk to the café to start work at six-thirty.

For her, the rush-hour, which in the morning lasted two and a half, was the worst part of the day; queues out the door, everyone wanting coffee, and always in the thirty seconds before the next train was due. It didn't help that the people at the back of the queue could see the digital display suspended above the platform and knew exactly how long that would be. It wasn't unusual, on days when one of the espresso machines broke down or if someone had a big or complicated order, for an entire queue of impatient customers to suddenly break ranks and run towards the station.

She also hated how rude people were. The same people who toddled off in their designer skirts and jackets, to-die-for shoes and beautiful tote bags, who probably had lovely, modern offices and went for fancy bistro lunches. She doubted many of them had to change a toxic nappy before they left home, or had people shout orders at them like they were retarded, or had to scrape cold leftover food into slop-bins without getting it under their pristinely-manicured nails. And she couldn't imagine *any* of them getting home in the late afternoon with aching legs and swollen feet, stinking of spent coffee grounds with the taste of cabbage-infused dishwasher fluid cloying at the back of their throat. But she told herself it could have been worse; by now, she probably would have been assigned to a ward, changing catheter bags, mopping up sick, and being spat at and abused. No, it wasn't her first choice career, but she had grown to love this job, especially after nine o'clock when the rush-hour was over.

That was when the normal people started coming in. Pensioners and carers, local builders and tradesmen, shop-workers and housewives—even the odd few househusbands, new mothers and dog-walkers—and the modern breed they called telecommuters, though weren't they supposed to be at home working? One thing set these people apart from the early crowd. They weren't in any hurry. They actually came in to spend time there and the more *they* enjoyed being there, the more Siobhan did. It was as close as she felt she could now come to fulfilling her dream of becoming a nurse.

And just now and again, someone walked in to make the day complete. She smiled at the thought of that cheeky guy yesterday, remembering his sexy swagger, low-hung jeans and over-sized trainers. The black hoodie, up over the white baseball cap, turned slightly to one side. His broad shoulders and dark eyes. And that gorgeous smile...

'Americano, please. None of that... froth.' It wasn't an unpleasant tone, but it was firm and uncompromising, snapping her from the daydream. Facing her across the counter was someone who clearly took their coffee seriously and she smiled back, in spite of his lack of eye contact. He was smartly dressed, in an old-fashioned way, and she noticed the brown hat in his hand that he must have taken off as he entered the café.

'You could always have it skinny,' she said, prompting the man to look up from unbuttoning his coat.

'Do I look like I'd want it skinny?' He scowled, until a raffish grin curled one side of his mouth. 'No, my dear. Just the coffee.'

'Take a seat,' she said. 'I'll bring it over.'

It had been a while since he was last in this café and he had only decided to come in that day because it was unusually quiet. With plenty of tables to choose from, he walked to the far end, put his hat and coat neatly on the opposite chair, and took a seat with his back to the wall.

From there, he could still see everyone come and go but, more than anything, he was hoping to be able to enjoy his own company for a change. Most of the people he had to deal with were fools, and sometimes it was nice to find somewhere out of the way where he could enjoy a few minutes of peace. Even so, old habits die hard, he mused, as he took his phone from inside his jacket and put it on the table. Before long, the waitress arrived with his coffee.

'Did you want anything to eat with that?' she asked, as she set down the steaming mug in front of him.

'Hmm... Go on then, surprise me,' he said, and she smiled back in delight.

'Well, there are still some savouries left, but if you wanted something sweet, we've got...'

'Something sweet,' he said. 'You choose.'

'O-kay,' she said, narrowing her eyes. 'I'll be right back.'

He watched her return to the counter and allowed himself a moment of weakness. He hadn't seen her in here before. He would have remembered that stunning auburn hair, just visible beneath the netting at the back of her obligatory white headwear. He guessed she was in her early twenties, and those two facts alone were enough to transport him back to a carefree summer, exploring the Kentish coast with Annie, the girl he thought he would never lose. But it was a thought conflicted with guilt and sadness for the other woman he had later married, only to lose her too.

Moments later, she was back with a plate and a smile. She'd chosen a slice of Victoria sponge and he nodded his approval.

***

In Chatham, Jam froze, neither able to move nor look away. The man standing over his friend's crumpled mound of a body was shorter and probably less than half Jabba's weight. As if he'd spent all his energy on that one merciless swing, he now dragged the baseball bat along the ground.

Jam's own pursuer had also slowed to watch, but now saw the chance to make up lost ground, and when Jam finally turned to notice him, the assailant was within striking distance.

Too late to see the upward thrust of the man's fist, Jam felt the impact of the haymaker connect with his jaw. His head jolted backwards and consciousness faltered momentarily like a neon light flickering in his brain. It had been many years since he had hit the canvas and his body refused to go over now. His feet shifted to counter the momentum, and when they buckled, his knees held strong. He heard the trainer scream in his ears. *Go down! Stay down!*

But there were no rules here to protect him if he did. No referee, no count to ten, no ringside paramedic. The pride and instinct that kept him from dropping held him cruelly at punch-ball height. Bare-knuckle blows sent his head back and forth, left and right, until he could take no more and he curled on the ground as toe-capped boots pummelled his body.

***

The plate had been scraped clean and the mug was empty when Siobhan returned to clear his table. He was deep in conversation on his phone, but she couldn't understand, let alone recognise, the foreign language he was speaking. Impressed, nonetheless, she placed the dirty crockery on the tray as quietly as she could and picked it up. When he held up his finger, she raised her head and saw that he had wrapped his other hand around the mouthpiece.

'Miss,' he said.

'Siobhan,' she whispered back, pointing to her name badge.

'Siobhan, could you bring another coffee. Please.'

'Same again, coming up. More cake?' she replied, and he shook his head and went back to his conversation.

He'd finished the call when she came back with his drink.

'I always wanted to speak another language,' she said, 'but I have enough trouble with this one.' She laughed.

'Oh, it's really not such a big deal,' he replied. 'When you spend some time in a foreign country, you'd be surprised how easy it is.'

'Which country was it?'

'Several...' he said, dismissively. 'In Asia Pacific mainly.'

'Business or pleasure?'

'You ask a lot of questions,' he said, and her smile dropped momentarily. 'But it's only right that I introduce myself, now that I know your name. I'm Herbert.'

She barely suppressed her snigger, which was in part because she hadn't met a Herbert before, and partly because he held out his hand. She stood there a moment, self-conscious, before beaming warmly and accepting the gesture.

'It's a pleasure to meet you... Herbert,' she said, shaking his hand, and this time her smile failed to mask the giggle.

'People who know me,' he said, 'call me Herb.'

'Well,' she said, nodding her approval, 'I suppose that means I can call you Herb too.'

'You may,' he said. 'I once knew a young lady with hair like yours.' She felt her cheeks flush, but before he could embarrass her further, his phone began buzzing as it set off on its own path across the table. He picked it up and looked at the screen, his expression changing. This time when he held up his hand, it was a dismissive gesture, and she nodded and turned to go.

'What is it?' The harsh tone he used to answer the call shocked her as she walked away to clear another table. Now, as she glanced back at him, his entire expression had changed. His pale features had tightened and he was staring into space, his voice now too low for her to hear. She shrugged and started heading towards the kitchen when another customer got up and left one of the tables along the back of the café. With space on her tray for another cup, she diverted towards it.

She didn't mean to listen, but she sensed he hadn't seen her approaching on his blindside and, with the nearby table now empty, he'd allowed his voice to rise.

'Two of them...?' he challenged. 'Both beaten...? How

badly?' Now she couldn't help but listen as he continued interrogating the messenger. 'You saw them, yes? Definitely still alive... Where did they take them?'

He now had his back to her as Siobhan put the empty mug on the tray and began polishing the table needlessly.

'You're sure it was them...? Bastards!' He spat out the curse and she looked over just as the back of his head shook. 'I need you to deal with this, Mac. I'm relying on you... Yes... whatever it takes... No one does a job for me that ends this way. Do you hear? Now, get them back and call me when you have.'

He ended the call abruptly and caught her off guard when he suddenly turned around before she could look away.

'Ah,' he said. 'You're still there.'

'Sorry, I...' she looked down at the table and reached to pick up the tray. 'I was just...'

'What did you hear?'

'I... er, nothing.'

'Seriously? So why are you looking at me like that?'

'Just that... it sounded like someone's been hurt.'

'Yes,' he said. 'But it's under control.'

'Hurt badly?'

'Just a lad who was working for me... had an accident. He'll be fine.'

'An accident... right. In that case, shouldn't you call an ambulance?'

'There's really no need for you to worry. They're not even around here.'

'They?' As she met his gaze, she gripped the tray and the mugs rattled.

His mouth curled upwards but his eyes remained set. 'The man I was talking to will bring him home.' His words were slow and the intensity of his stare now overshadowed the forced smile.

She sensed he'd drawn a line and she stood momentarily, contemplating her retreat. Instead, she took another step towards it. 'You said two of them.'

He straightened his back, taking in a deep breath. 'Well... don't you have big ears,' he said, and a muscle in his temple twitched.

'And you said they've been beaten.' She crossed the line.

He exhaled loudly. 'Your concern is admirable. But you really need to step away now.'

'Shouldn't we call the police?'

'That won't be necessary,' he said, and held her in his glare before dropping his eyes back to the phone in his hand.

She looked around anxiously; the café was still almost empty and her boss was busy refilling shelves behind the counter. 'Whatever it takes,' she said. 'That's what you told *him*.'

'And that's what he'll do.' His words now came out lead-lined and she blanched and walked back to the kitchen.

***

The other watcher moved away from the heavily-tinted window and back into the driving seat of the white van that had sat brazenly all morning in the car park of the Chatham industrial estate compound. Having received new instructions, he flipped his phone shut and started the engine. He'd already written down the number plate of the black 4x4 into which the two unconscious men had been bundled moments before and, after watching it drive away, set out in cautious pursuit.

***

How much later, he didn't know, but Jam tried to open his eyes. He'd already attempted to move his hands but they were pinned beneath his body, and the skin on his wrists pinched when he tried to twist them apart. Now he was trying to work out if his eyes wouldn't open because they couldn't or because something else was stopping them. He got the answer when he lifted his head and got the same sensation of adhesive, pulling at his hair.

His mouth was similarly held shut but he found there was

some give in the tape and he started working at the gap by moving his jaw. The pain that shot through his brain reminded him of the beating he'd taken and he moved his mouth more slowly until he could finally extend his top teeth over his lip and get some grip on the sticky surface. All the time he worked at this slightest glimmer of hope, he was aware only of the smell of fish and diesel.

When he stopped momentarily, the sound that met his ears was a low gurgle like a dual-outlet drain siphoning. It was close by and he swivelled his hips and swept his conjoined feet left and right until he found resistance and the noise stopped... only to start up a few seconds later. By now, Jam was able to open his mouth and with one last painful stretch of his jaw, the tape came away from his top lip.

'Jabba!' His whispered shout was met with a grunt and that was all he needed to renew his strength.

'Is okay, blood,' he said. 'I'll get you outta dis.' With that, he started wrenching his hands apart, ignoring the pain in his shoulders and the ripping of hair from his arms.

He managed to stretch the tape a little, but it just became thinner so that each twist burned deeper into his flesh. Having to contend with his own body weight was exhausting what little energy he had. But when he rolled onto his side, away from where he knew his friend lay badly injured, he found that he could bend his knees right up to his chest. Apart from the relief he felt in his back, he realised that the tape around his wrists was now loose enough to allow his hands to slip under his feet. At the second attempt, they scraped beneath his trainers and he was able to twist his arms on the way up so that, at the expense of more hair, the tape split and he exhaled deeply as his wrists parted company. It was only after carefully teasing the layers of tape over the ridge of his skull, hoping to at least leave some of his eyebrows intact, that he finally allowed his head to drop back to the ground in a moment of triumphant exhaustion.

The sense of relief in opening his eyes was short-lived because the space was pitch-black. He reached out in the darkness and found Jabba's chubby hand. It felt cold and lifeless to his touch; he held onto it tightly. The sound of breathing slowed and for a moment, Jam's heart sank, but then he felt the stubby fingers twitch and close loosely around his own.

'You gonna be alright, Jabba. We gonna be alright, bruv.'

***

Terry Pinner kept a private pay-as-you-go phone in his jacket pocket. Its number was known only to a select group of his contacts. When it started to vibrate, he stepped away from his desk.

'Tel, it's George Harris,' the familiar voice said when he answered. 'All clear this end. Everything's in order and we've settled with the driver. And Ray is well pleased. Your slate is clean, my friend. Even sends his regards to the wife... Gillian, I think he said, yeah? And to your two lovely kids. Anyway, wanted me to tell you to get in touch if you get any more stuff like that. Quality gear. Another one of those, Tel, and you'll be back on the payroll.'

Pinner returned the phone to his inner jacket pocket, pulled open the door from the stairwell and stepped back into the office.

'Guv?'

He almost jumped out of his skin when the young female constable in his team called across to him as he entered. 'What?' he bellowed back, and the room went quiet.

'Tea or coffee?' she asked, with a forced smile.

4.

'What's occurring, Siobhan?' It was Brian, her Welsh boss, who sang out as he came up to her in the staff room. 'You look like you've seen a ghost.'

'That man,' she said, and her eyes squinted in the direction of the door to the café.

'What, Mr Angry?'

'You know him?'

'Been comin' in here for years, he has.'

'Why do you call him that?'

'Just my little joke. I can never remember his surname, sounds something like that, anyway.'

'He said his name's Herb.'

'Oh, I dunno. Nice chap though. What did he say to you?'

'Well, yeah. He was being very nice, but then he got a call... and suddenly, he's gone a bit... I don't know, funny with me.'

'Do you want me to go and talk to him, presh?'

'No. Maybe it's nothing. It sounds like there's been some trouble. Some men have been hurt, but he won't call the police or get them an ambulance.'

'Come on, Siobhan,' he said, his tone changing. 'We talked about this. You can't go getting involved in every customer's little ups and downs. I know it's been difficult for you, but you know what 'appened last month when you tried to help that little, old lady.'

'What? I thought she'd slipped on the ice outside. I told you to put grit down,' she said, as Brian folded his arms and held his head on one side. 'How was I supposed to know she was still holding her purse through the grille?'

'She was... until you rolled her over and she dropped it

41

down the drain.' He shook his head. 'Three cups of tea and a cheesecake that cost me before she calmed down.'

'Anyway, that was different,' she said.

'Look,' he said, 'if you're worried, why don't you offer to take a look at them? It's not like you don't know what you're doing.'

'I'm not even sure where they are.'

'Sounds like you need to leave it then,' he said, nodding his head. 'Why don't you go and take him another coffee, on the house, when he's finished that one, and forget all about it?'

***

As his eyes started to adjust, Jam could make out he was in some kind of lock-up. What little light there was originated from the back, behind several layers of stacked crates. Removing Jabba's gag became a priority, because Jam knew his friend was likely to vomit, and there was every chance he would choke on it. Having untied him, he leant him against the side wall and started feeling his way along to the darker end of the rectangular void.

The cold touch of a metal up-and-over door told him this was probably a large garage-style pre-fab. He pushed against the inner frame but there was no movement. The simple vertical bolt that usually provided minimal security to this type of door had been supplemented with something far more robust.

After inching his way to the other end, he started dragging the heavy containers into the middle of the space. Being careful not to stack them precariously, he got to the final layer that stood between him and what must have been an opening of sorts, and when daylight poured around the side of the next box he moved, his spirits lifted.

The bad news was that the window, being no more than a long skylight positioned six feet from the floor and with a single fixed pane less than a foot deep, reinforced with wire mesh, was, as escape routes go, completely useless. At least Jam was able to look through it from the top of a crate, but the view simply confirmed his suspicion: a gravel track lay between him and another row of identical concrete prefabs that extended out of sight in both directions.

Jabba was awake, but not very lucid when Jam went back to check on him. He'd been sick, but at least now that daylight filled the room, Jam could see there was colour in his face and he seemed to be able to focus his eyes. He sat down and put an arm around his friend's shoulders, and they sat together for a long time in silence.

Teasing the thin end of the crowbar beneath the metal lip, the man Herb called Mac prepared to lever his full weight against the door. The first time it slipped, and his knuckles crunched into the gravel under the force of his own substantial momentum. He cursed, brushed the stones from his bleeding skin and repositioned the bar to try again.

Jam pulled Jabba further from the door as they heard the clash of metal. Jabba tried to get up to help himself move along, but the lights flickered in his head and he projected more bile onto the concrete. Rather than trying to move him again, Jam dragged one of the crates so that it stood between his friend and the door. He then looked around in desperation for something to protect them with. But he already knew all the crates were sealed and there was nothing else lying around, so he reverted to the only other weapons he could rely on and raised his fists.

Mac leaned again on the jemmy-bar but he was beginning to realise something wasn't normal about this door. Its bottom bolt should have pinged out of the hole in the ground by now but the door itself had hardly moved, save for a slight upward crease in the lip of its lower edge. He studied the sides, looking for signs of lateral bolts, but if there were any, they were set far enough back that he couldn't see them. And if he couldn't see them, he couldn't get to them with the tool he had. All he could do was re-position the bar and keep trying.

43

When the door slid upwards, Jam was momentarily blinded by the afternoon sunshine. In the split second it took him to put one hand in front of his eyes, he felt the full force of a rugby tackle around his waist. He didn't recognise the bonehead who attacked him, but even before he hit the ground, Jam reacted viciously and unleashed a ballistic array of punches. His attacker lost the advantage and rolled away stunned. In no time, Jam was back on his feet and aimed a kick that landed sweetly behind the thug's ear and his head cannoned hard against the wall.

Jam didn't wait to see if he moved again because he could hear there was another guy outside. Yet when he spun back towards the garage door, it was already too late; a heavy chain hit his legs and wrapped itself around his knees. He went to ground heavily and caught a glimpse of this unknown assailant dragging him along the concrete out into the daylight. But this time when the sunshine dazzled him, it was short-lived because a dark, looming shape put him back into shadow.

Mac had rounded the corner from the wrong row of garages and ran at the man he saw dragging Jam by a chain around his knees. The impact sent the man face first into the gravel and the chain unravelled from Jam's legs. By the time the man looked up, stones embedded in his forehead, Mac was on him, wrapping the chain around his neck. He didn't release it until the man's tongue lolled from his mouth and even then, he seemed to hold it longer than was necessary.

Jam turned away, grateful just to be alive and headed back in to check on the other assailant. That man was crumpled against the wall and whilst he might have still been breathing, he wasn't going anywhere soon. One quick look at both meatheads, with their shaven skulls, thick-set necks and muscular arms told Jam these were not the men who had brought them here. Jabba peered around the side of the crate and Jam went to him.

'Who dat?' Jabba said.

'Fockin' Bre'vart!' Jam whispered.

'Oh, okay man,' Jabba said, as if that was perfectly feasible. 'I fink I can stand up now.' Jam leaned down to help him but was

44

shunted aside by Mac who scooped his arm under Jabba's bulk and led him out into the fresh air. Jam scowled as he stepped back out into the sunshine but Mac pushed past him again, dragging the lifeless body back into the lock-up by the chain still attached to its neck. Jam sat with Jabba on the ground outside and watched in stunned silence as Mac unravelled the chain and then wrapped it around the second man's neck, silently killing him in cold blood.

***

When the call finally came, Herb had finished his second Americano and his head was starting to buzz.

'Got them,' were the only words he needed to hear, but he listened intently to the rest.

'Nice work, Mac,' he said. 'Bring them back up here and I'll take a look at them. If the fat boy needs attention, it'll probably be better to get it up here. And if they need to sleep it off, we can sort something out.'

He returned the phone to his pocket and got up to leave.

'On the house,' Siobhan said, and put another fresh coffee on the table, having caught him offside once again. He sat back down.

'Thank you.'

'How is the... fat boy?' She stared but he didn't look up.

'Hopefully nothing serious.'

'Now will you call the police?' She raised her voice.

'Definitely not,' he said, his tone uncompromising, as he looked around the empty café. 'Especially not now.'

'But they might need a doctor,' she said.

'We'll cross that bridge when we come to it.'

'Well, let me take a look at them,' she said, and he finally looked at her.

'Absolutely not,' he said firmly, before adding more conciliatorily, 'Like I said, you're better staying out of this.'

'I can help, honestly.'

'Really,' he smirked. 'You're just a...'

'Waitress?' She put her hands on her hips and raised her eyebrows. 'You know, I haven't always been serving coffee and clearing tables.'

'So, what are you?' He didn't want to ridicule this young girl; he quite liked her. But she was starting to push her luck. 'St John's volunteer? Resident first aider?'

'Hmm,' she scowled back. 'Something like that.'

He pursed his lips and held her gaze. 'Out of the question,' he said and reached for his coat.

But she hadn't finished. She leaned down so that her face was at the side of his head and whispered in his ear. 'If you don't let me see them, I'm calling the police, now.'

He turned his head and she felt his bristles scuff her cheek as she pulled back. 'Okay, Siobhan,' he said, calmly looking into her eyes. 'If you're sure that's the way you want to play this. But don't say I didn't warn you.'

It was only mid-afternoon and she knew there was a risk her dad wouldn't be up yet. He used an answering machine to field daytime calls and when it cut in, she assumed he was sleeping and left an obscure message to the effect that she had to pop out for the evening to see a friend. She was then surprised how quickly he'd phoned her back, having already made arrangements for the childminder to keep Eloise overnight, and reassured her it wasn't a problem, she deserved more freedom.

The truth of the matter was that it also eased his conscience, for her to have time away from effectively being the child's surrogate. She gratefully accepted the arrangements and offered to make it up by babysitting at the weekend so that he could continue the search for her mother.

'Are you sure about this, Siobhan?' Brian said after she asked him if she could leave early.

'He is a bit scary,' she said, looking across towards Herb, who was still sitting at the table, reluctantly waiting for her.

'I don't mean *him*. Old-school that one, trust me.' Brian had lived in the bustling London borough for the best part of twenty years, but still saw the world through unsuspecting eyes, as if back in the rural neighbourhood where he grew up in The Valleys. 'I'm pretty sure I met his wife, once... long time ago, mind. Lovely woman. Model, I think she was.'

'So what's there to worry about?' she said, largely for her own reassurance.

'You can't heal all the world's problems, that's all I'm saying. It's bad enough... what with everything else... and the baby and all.' He put his hand on hers. 'But I suppose if he's asked you to come and look at them, he must be worried.'

'Yeah. I'll be fine,' she said.

'You've got your alarm in your bag, 'ave you? And make sure you text me when you get home.'

'Okay,' she agreed. 'He said it's only a couple of minutes around the corner. And if I don't feel comfortable with anything, I'll ring you, alright?'

'Okay. But I want you here bright-eyed and bushy-tailed in the morning, you hear?'

'Yes,' she said, brightening up. 'I might even be early. And with Eloise having a sleepover, I...' she said with a grin, 'can even have a lie-in!'

'Go on then,' he said, and she blew him a kiss and went to get her coat.

True to his word, Herb led her to the house within minutes of leaving the café. There was no sight of the van he had mentioned would be arriving soon, as they walked along the street. The road itself seemed pleasant enough; she'd driven along it several times but had never stopped or taken much notice of the houses.

They were mainly semi-detached and well-kept with tidy front gardens and, for that time on a weekday, those cars that were parked on the driveways suggested an average, middle-class environment. That was until he held out his hand towards a gateless opening onto the front garden of a house that, at first sight, nestled unnoticed among its neighbours, but when viewed in isolation, stood out for several reasons. Notably, it was the only detached house on that side of the road, and its obvious state of poor repair was only thinly disguised by the rampant ivy that clung to its outer walls.

She looked at him askance, but he nodded unapologetically and she found herself walking, now with greater trepidation, towards the front door. Once inside, he ushered her into the room on the right, giving her the distinct impression, despite his apparent indifference, that he really didn't want her to get a good look around. She'd lived in some basic accommodation as a student, but nothing came close to what she had just walked into. He flicked the light switch and a single clear bulb laid bare the room's absent charm with its intense, shade-less glare. The room was virtually empty, apart from two ancient armchairs, an electric fire set into the cavity of an old hearth and an even older-looking bureau in the far corner. Only the ripped lining of the drapes that hung from a pitted brass pole over the window touched the bare wooden floor, and they wafted a strong, musty smell as he pulled them together, despite the remaining hours of daylight beyond.

'When they arrive,' she began tentatively, 'where can we...'

'There's a bed across the hall,' he said. 'I realise this isn't... ideal.'

'What is this place?'

'It's just a place,' he replied. 'We're doing it up... out the back. One of these lads... had been helping out.'

'So what's really happened to them?'

'They were doing another job for me...'

She shot him another question before he could elaborate. 'What, more building work? In another place... like this?'

'No, no. Nothing like that. It was, er... a watching brief, you might say. No one was supposed to get hurt.'

'Look, you can stop playing with me now,' she said, and he recoiled visibly from her sudden frankness. 'It's pretty obvious this isn't all completely legit. Otherwise, they'd be in hospital.'

'Well,' he said, composing himself. 'That all depends on your viewpoint. We were merely protecting our business interests. And if they need the hospital, that's where they'll go. That's what you're here to decide.'

'Well, we'll have to see about that.'

'Brian assured me you could help,' he said, and her eyebrows shot up.

'Did he?'

'But... I don't take kindly to blackmail.'

'Yeah, well I'm sorry about that,' she said, and suddenly felt strangely at ease. 'Maybe you can start by telling me what we're dealing with? When they get here... what state are they in?'

'The one I know could look after himself; his are just cuts and bruises. It's the other one I know nothing about. It seems he took a blow to the head.'

'That could be serious.'

'We'll soon see, but at least he's conscious.'

'That doesn't mean a thing.'

'No,' he said with a sombre nod. 'I'm well aware of that.'

5.

After an uncomfortable silence, Siobhan felt ready to take the initiative. 'Tell me you have something I can use to treat them with,' she said, looking around the room doubtfully. 'Cotton wool, bandages...'

'I'll have a look.' Herb stood up to leave the room.

'And some boiling water,' she added, before deciding to go with him. She at least wanted to see where she was going to be assessing these walking wounded. But before she followed him out, she pulled back the curtain. The traffic was starting to increase as the evening rush beckoned, and several cars were making slow progress past the house. Behind them, she saw a white van indicating to pull in.

'Is this them?' she called down the hall as she unlatched the front door. The van had now managed to pull into the space at the dipped kerbside in front of the opening to the house and she rushed out to meet it. The man who pulled his colossal frame out of the driver's seat ignored her as he went around to the rear doors. When she followed him, he was about to turn on her, when Herb shouted from the house.

'She's here to help, Mac. Let her see them.'

He grunted as he opened the doors and when he stepped onto the tail-plate, the van lurched back on its suspension. When he reappeared, he was hunched over a younger man whose short stature belied a stout frame. With an arm looped awkwardly around the injured man's back and a huge hand cradling his armpit, Mac guided him out and virtually carried him to the wall where he waited for a second. The younger man's face was pale and there was blood in his hair, which Siobhan tried to take a look at, but Mac dismissed her fussing and continued moving him along the pavement.

'What about the other one?' she asked.

'Fock him!' he said, and continued to manhandle the little, fat man towards the gateway. Before she could fathom his obvious disdain for the other casualty, he virtually dragged the one he did seem to care about along the path to where Herb helped them both squeeze improbably through the front door and into the house.

'Don't worry 'bout Bre'vart!' It was an unexpectedly perky remark that came from behind her, and a voice not altogether unfamiliar, and she turned to see her cheeky customer from yesterday stepping down from the van. The handsome face that had turned her head was still smiling but there were swellings under both eyes and the line of his jaw was already turning purple.

'Oh my God!' she said. 'I had no idea it was you.'

'Nice to see you,' he said, and the surprise was complete when she put an arm around his shoulder and gave him a gentle, little hug. He winced with the pain in his ribs, and as she pulled away, his face accidentally brushed against her cheek and he breathed in her perfume.

He said he was okay to walk but she kept her arm around him as they went inside the house. When she let him go, he leaned against the doorframe of the front room. She could hear Herb talking with his associate in the room diagonally to the left, and she crossed the hall and walked in. By now, she had lost interest in the state of the place and sat down on the bed beside the man with blood matted in his hair and lowered his head for a better look. She'd noticed how the conversation stopped abruptly when she came in and the two older men left the room and continued to speak in hushed tones in the hall. Then she heard the front door close and Herb reappeared at the door.

'Did you get some hot water?' she asked, and he nodded. 'I take it you have a bowl and some *clean* cloth I can bathe the wound with?' Her emphasis on the word clean caused Herb to nod sagely.

'Yes,' he said. 'There's a first aid kit the builder left behind. I'll bring it through.'

'I'm Siobhan,' she said, standing up so her patient could see her without turning too quickly. 'Can you tell me your name?'

'Dat ma bruvver, Jabba.' The answer came from the other casualty, who was now standing in the doorway. 'An' I'm Jam.'

'Okay, Jam,' she said. 'Thank you, but I really need Jabba to answer some questions for me first.'

'You a nurse?' he said.

'No, I... ' She looked at him and frowned. 'I trained... but I had to stop.'

'You know what ya doin', dough?'

'Well, up to a point. I can clean it and take a look. But if he needs proper medical care, we need to get him to a hospital.' She looked from one to the other. 'And how about you? How are you feeling?'

'Don't worry bout me, I've had worse dan dis. Just make sure he's okay, yeah?'

'Jabba,' she said, turning back to face him, 'I need you to look up at me...'

Jam left her to it and went to find Herb out in the back room. The refit was now finished and as he passed through the new breeze-block corridor, Jam noticed the locks and bolts that had been added to the heavy doors after his untimely departure. Herb was standing at an old ceramic sink, pouring boiling water from the kettle into an equally crazed pudding bowl on the drainer. He swirled the steaming water and poured it away before refilling it and setting it down alongside the first aid kit. Jam watched as Herb looked through the contents of the kit and picked out the sterilised pack of wadding.

'Who were dose guys?' Jam asked, and Herb stopped and looked around, slightly fazed by the sudden question.

'You didn't need to know,' he replied, but Jam wasn't having that.

'You givin' me jokes, man? Dey almost kill us.'

'What did I say?' Herb said, but he wasn't looking for an

answer. 'I told you not to get involved...'

'We didn't...' Jam tried to protest, but Herb wasn't finished.

'And *not* to tell a living soul,' he continued, his voice echoing through the house. 'If you hadn't taken that... tub of lard with you...'

'Ay! Dat's liber'ies, old man,' Jam shouted back and, just then, Siobhan appeared at the door.

'Can you two do this later?' she said. 'Only this isn't helping Jabba.'

'I'm sorry,' Herb said and Jam mumbled his own apology.

'What do you think?' Herb asked.

'He seems reasonably alert, but just a bit...'

'What?' said Jam.

'Slow?' she said with a frown.

'You know dat,' Jam nodded back.

Herb shot him a look of fuming bewilderment that Siobhan read as no more than a prefix to a further tirade. She guessed his next words would probably be, '*In that case, what the hell...*' so she over-ruled them before they were out of his mouth.

'Now that's enough. Bring those things through,' she said, and walked back out into the passageway. She was too focused on her patient to even notice the metal doors and heavy-duty combination locks, let alone to wonder what was behind them.

Herb carried the water and wadding pack, and Jam gathered up the rest of the first aid kit and they followed her out. Jabba was still sitting on the bed and Siobhan sat alongside him. She took the wadding from Herb and opened the seal.

'I'll stay wiv him,' Jam said, and took the bowl from Herb who nodded and left the room.

At first, the blood started flowing again as Siobhan gently dabbed at the wound, but as the crust around it was slowly washed away, her concern receded.

'So, you don't remember what it was that hit your head?'

Jabba shrugged and looked at Jam.

'He didn't see it comin', man,' Jam said. 'I fink it was a baseball bat.'

Siobhan winced and continued to bathe and inspect the wound for several minutes, and Jam stood in silence, holding the water that was now dark red.

'Well, at least it's a clean cut and there doesn't seem to be a fracture,' she finally said before standing to face the patient. 'Jabba, remember what we said?'

'If I feel sick, I let you know.'

'What else?'

'Or faint... or dizzy.'

'Well done. How do you feel now?'

'Tired man.'

'I know, Jabba. But we need to keep you sitting upright and I want you to stay awake for me, okay. Do you think you can do that?'

'I'll do it for you, baby,' he said and winked at her.

She smiled.

'Don't go gettin' no ideas, bruv,' Jam said, and his mate grinned back, sheepishly.

Siobhan took a roll of bandage from the kit and broke into the packaging, and did the same with a square of gauze and began to dress the wound. When Jam came back with clean water, she had finished pinning a bandage in place around Jabba's head. Jam helped lift his friend's feet onto the bed while Siobhan bundled up the cover behind the old pillow so that Jabba could sit upright. She took the clean water and started dabbing the slit in his chin with fresh wadding.

'I'll sit wiv him,' Jam said, after she'd finished cleaning and dressing the cut. 'To make sure he don't go sleep.'

'No, you're alright,' she said. 'I'd like to keep an eye on him a bit longer. I'd also like to take a look at you.'

'Dis is nuffink.' He rubbed his chin and stretched his chest, wincing when he breathed out. 'Jus' look out for ma bruvver, yeah.'

'Okay... for now,' she said, shaking her head. 'But once I'm happy with Jabba, I'm going to look at those ribs.'

'For real.'

'Go on,' she said, glancing through the doorway into the hall, 'it sounds like you've got unfinished business to discuss.'

'Yeah man. Wouldn't you?'

'Not my concern,' she said. 'I was trained not to judge or take sides. You can't get drawn into the reasons.'

'But...'

'No. It's the only way you can stay detached and ensure every patient gets the care they need, no matter what might have brought them through the door.'

'Yeah, I get dat,' he said, still slightly disappointed that she wasn't ready to take his side. 'Why did you stop... da trainin', you know?'

'That's a long story.' One she wasn't going to start now.

'Tell me some time,' he said, and she smiled back. 'You would be a proper good nurse.'

'Thank you,' she said. 'Now, please, just keep it down in there, yeah?'

'Yeah man.'

When Jam walked into the front room, Herb was seated in one of the armchairs. The electric fire was alight, but there was a damp chill in the air.

'How is he?' Herb asked.

'She's wiv him. He's safe man.' Jam crossed the room, stretching his arms, and yawned.

'Best to keep watching. Head injury like that... I've seen it before.' Herb tailed off, looking down at his hands clasped in his lap.

''Bout wh'appen, man,' Jam said. He held his stomach and grimaced as he lowered himself into the other chair.

'Yes, I *am* sorry, but...'

'Yeah, I know.' Jam sighed. 'I shouldna involved him.'

'You were lucky. It could have been much worse. If Mac hadn't been there.'

'Yeah man. How did *he* know... where we were?'

'I sent him,' Herb said. 'He's already told me everything.'

'Dat's deep.' Jam slumped back in the seat.

'As it turned out, I think we can all be grateful. But, it wasn't that I didn't trust you. I just started having second thoughts. We got a tip-off about the lorry. There'd been some kind of diversion. Something wasn't right. And for a big guy, he's got a knack of going unnoticed, so it was no more than an insurance policy.'

'For who man? Not for me and my bruv, Jabba.'

'He got you out of it, didn't he?' Herb said, before adding, 'He always gets the job done.'

'But da way he kill dose men...'

'Rather that than the alternative.'

'Dat's proper cold man,' Jam said with a sigh, gently rubbing the swelling in his jaw.

'And don't forget, he's not exactly your number one fan... after yesterday.'

'Yeah, but he arksed for dat. He was bein' a bully and dat's one fing I ain't standin' for.'

'I'm just saying, watch yourself, he's still seething and he holds a grudge like a circus lion.'

'But he still rescue us, yeah.'

'Fortunately for me, he's also very loyal. And that's probably the only thing stopping him from coming after you.'

'Where is he now?'

'Doing what he does best. Cleaning up the mess you left behind.'

Jam dug into his front pocket and took out a crumpled packet. When the only cigarette came out in two crushed pieces, he tossed it onto the floor and the two men sat in awkward silence.

'What was in dat lorry, wurf killin' for?' Jam was the first to speak but he didn't wait for an answer. 'I saw it come and it went frough okay, jus' like you said. If ev'ryfink in it was destroy, dat's what you want, yeah? So da nex' man couldn't get it?'

'There'd already been a switch... before it even got to Chatham.'

'Your stuff didn't get burn?'

'No, my... stock is still out there.'

'Uh-uh,' Jam said, raising his eyebrows. He was starting to get the picture. 'And dem clowns what jump us, dey got it now? Dere's bare wooden crates in dat garage.'

'No, that wouldn't have been it. And I don't know who those knuckle-heads were but I've got a fair idea who's behind it. The question is how did *he* know it was even up for grabs?'

'Who's *he*?'

'His name's Riggs, he's a slime-ball.' Herb scowled, his face rigid with contempt. 'He took something from me once before. And one day I'm going to kill him for it.'

'For real, if you know da man...' Jam said, but when Herb's eyes narrowed dismissively, the penny dropped. 'You said it was a safe place, yeah?'

'Exactly. It's where they get rid of confiscated gear. It was the police who had it.'

'So dey da ones what lost it.'

'Or gave it away.'

'An inside job?'

'I think you're catching on.'

'What we gonna do 'bout it?'

'We?'

'What dey jus' did to ma blood, Jabba... I ain't never walk away from a fight...' Herb frowned, but Jam's face clenched and he shook his head. 'Dis was diff'rent. Dat bastard get a touch... jus' a lucky punch. Dey was proper bait, man. Jabba don't... we don't do nuffink for what dey do to us. And da ones what did it... dey still out dere.'

'Fair point. It's best you now know what we're up against.'

'So, wha-gwun, cuz? An wha's wiv dose new rooms, man?'

'You deserve to know everything. But on one condition.'

'Yeah?' Jam sat forward.

'Leave Jabba out...'

The sound of heavy thudding and Siobhan calling for help cut him off. They both jumped up and rushed from the room.

6.

Jabba's substantial bulk was thrashing about on the floor and Siobhan was on top, pinning him down. At first, Jam thought his bro had been trying it on with the pretty nurse, but not only was that completely out of character, his rapid blinking and entirely white eyes told him this was far more serious.

'Try to stop him moving!' she was screaming. 'We need to keep his head still!'

Between the three of them, Herb at his feet, Jam across his chest and arms and Siobhan at his head, they held him down for what seemed like minutes until the waves of violent shuddering became less frequent. Eventually, when Siobhan raised his eyelids, his pupils were visible again, but he had lost consciousness and she rolled him onto his side and positioned his arms and legs as she'd been taught.

'We need an ambulance,' she said.

'It'll take too long,' Herb countered. 'I can get to Whipps Cross quicker in the car. Give me a minute and I'll bring it round.' Before they could challenge him, he'd left the house.

'I don't know if we can even get him up,' Siobhan said, as she gently cradled his head and tried but failed to lift his shoulders.

'Got to,' Jam said, and grabbed the cover from the bed. 'Slide him to da front door for when da car comes.'

Herb risked the immaculate paintwork on his new Mercedes when he reversed it through the gap in the old fence, where a wooden gate designed for walk-in access had long since rotted away. The three of them then struggled to manoeuvre the dead weight of Jabba's bulk through the doorframe and into the back seat.

'One of us should come with you,' Siobhan said to Herb, but he waved her back.

'No. You stay here with him. Make sure he doesn't have a similar reaction. I'll ring the house phone to let you know.'

'I'm okay man,' Jam said. 'I should come wiv you.'

'No way. If you two arrive together, and you with a face like that... No, it's best if we try to keep this low key for now. I can say this was an accident.'

'But...'

'Besides, this wasn't your fault. And I'll be damned if I let this happen again.'

Before they could argue further, or even make sense of his final words, Herb was back in the car and with his hazard lights flashing, he pulled away and weaved through the queue of cars along the road towards the main junction.

Back in the house, they found the phone on the bureau and with nothing else to do but worry and wait, they sat down in the front room.

'It sounds like you've been here before,' Siobhan said, taking out cigarettes and a lighter from her purse. 'What is this place?'

'We was workin' on da rooms out dere, yeah,' he said, nodding to accept her offer and eagerly sliding a Mayfair out of the packet. 'Da guy what took me on kept ev'ryfink to himself. I fink he was scared of... dese guys. Don't like me arksin' too many questions. Jus' wanna do what dey say an' get paid.'

'I can't blame him for that,' she said and lit the cigarettes. 'But, doesn't it all seem a bit odd to you?'

'For real.'

'But the clothes... and that car. What's he doing living in a place like this?'

'No one lives here... Except Bre'vart, maybe.'

'Who?'

'Da big guy.'

'He called him Mac.'

'Yeah, whatever!'

'Don't be like that. I thought he saved your life.'

'I fink he would leave me dere if he could. I proper fronted him before.'

'Why was that?'

'Don't arks.'

'Okay. But tell me what happened today.' She scanned the room for something to use as an ashtray before looking down at the grubby floorboards and deciding a bit of ash wouldn't even be noticed.

'Fought you don't take sides.'

'Who said I'm going to judge? But until that phone rings, we've got nothing better to do.'

'Yeah.' He followed her gaze across the room and nodded. 'It was a proper hijack. Me an' Jabba were dere jus' to watch. But it was like someone knew. Da guy dat come for me, walk right up like dere's a big arrow on da door. Haha. He wasn't expectin' what he got.'

'Really? Sounds like the old, *you should see the other guy* story, judging by the state of your face.'

'I can look after maself, man. I woulda got away wivout a scratch. Dat's for real.'

'Seriously?' She winced as she continued staring at the swelling around his eyes.

'To start wiv, yeah, he come in, an' I'm like uh-uh, you know. Frontin' me wiv dis big-arse spanner in his hand. He try spark me wiv it. Not havin' dat, man, no way. He drop it when I tump him one time, right jab. Anuvver jab den a lef' hook, proper heavy, man. He go down, an' I'm like, "*Laters*". An' I run, yeah. Leadin' any uvvers away from ma bredder. He's safe, yeah, cos I tell him don't move till I come get you.'

'So, what went wrong?'

'I see him outta ma eye. Not hidin' no more.'

'Jabba?'

'Yeah, man... He fink he can help me. But it's like dey know where he is too. I see da guy behind him... bring him down wiv

61

his own clumsy feet... Den swing dat bat... Man, he's already bleedin', he ain't gettin' up. Dat's proper liber'ies man.'

'I'm sorry, Jam.'

'After he drop... Dunno wh'appen... I'm pullin' a whitey or sumfink, like I'm gonna puke. Den da uvver bastard, he's behind me, yeah... liber'ies, man. Liber'ies.'

'You're really close, aren't you?'

He sighed deeply and took a moment to compose himself. 'Ma mum used to babysit for him. Not dat he was a baby, yeah, but... sumfink went wrong, when he was born. His mum was never well again, she blame herself. He's two years older dan me, but he was kep back at school so we in da same class. No one else wanna sit by him.'

'He's lucky to have found a friend like you,' she said with a gentle smile.

'Not quick enough, dough,' he said, and her eyes narrowed, encouraging him to explain. It was a story he'd never told another person and this didn't feel like the time or place to start, but he found her green eyes drawing him in. Before he could stop himself, his words took him right back to the place where Jabba had received his last beating, at the hands of a gang of kids who'd made his first thirteen years a life of abject misery.

Jam had found him slumped backwards over an old wire and spindle fence with his fat arms pulled behind him, wedged between the dowels, his armpits stretching back over the twisted metal top rail and his wrists wrapped in the rusty loops at the bottom where the wood had rotted away. His white belly was sagging over the waistband of his soiled underpants, and his school clothes were scattered in shreds on the ground. His face was pulp.

Siobhan's hand was over her mouth and her eyes were fixed on Jam's.

'I undo him from da fence an' cover him up. Den I run home for help,' he said. 'After dat, we like... bruvvers. No one ever hit him since... till today.'

'You're not from around here, are you?' she asked and he

shook his head. 'So, what brought you here?'

'Dere was some trouble, back home. Free years ago. Some of dem boys grow up, an' dey wanna get even. Ma muvva say I had to stay wiv her sista. I don't wanna leave Jab behind but his mum need him dere.' He tailed off momentarily, and now she sensed he was holding back, but she could hardly criticise. His voice lowered as he continued. 'She was not good. Drinkin' too much, an' stoned a lot... deep man. Not long she call an' arks me to look after her boy. I say no problem, he's my bredren, man. But I dunno what she mean. I never fink she gonna do dat to herself.'

Siobhan went across to give him a hug.

'Jabba now in a council place an' get help wiv stuff. S'close to ma aun'ie's an' I can still look out for him,' he said, as she gently cradled his head in her arms.

What he didn't tell her was that he still kept a list of those boys' names. Two of the eight hadn't made it into adulthood. He'd never been challenged to explain what responsibility he may have had for that. As far as he was concerned, they both had it coming and when it came, it was a fair fight. At least it was on his side; the only weapons *he* used were his fists. Although another five of them had paid their dues in other ways, the risk of further recriminations could never be completely ignored. For that reason, Croydon was still a no-go zone. There was only one name scribbled in pencil on that tattered piece of paper waiting to be crossed through. The ringleader had disappeared off Jam's radar several years before. His name was Carlton Parr.

After she wiped his face with fresh water and wadding from the kitchen, she inspected his bruises, which thankfully, unlike Jabba's, looked a lot worse than they were; the damage was superficial.

'Have you eaten much today?' she said.

'Coffee,' he replied.

'Oh my God, I'll get you something.' She stood up and then stopped midway to the door. 'Do you think there's any food in this house?'

'Dunno,' he said. 'We had to bring our own sugar, dough.'

'Great!' She sat back down. 'Right, as soon as that phone rings and we know where we stand with Jabba, I'm going up the chippie.'

'No bacon an' eggs den?' he said, and they both laughed. 'For real, dough, don't you need to get home... to da baby?'

'No, I'm okay,' she replied. 'Daddy made arrangements with the childminder tonight, so I've got the evening off.'

'Her daddy?' he said, but she missed the question mark in his voice. 'Is... dat why you never finish da trainin'?'

'Yes,' she said, quietly, and he waited for her to elaborate, but she didn't.

Before he could probe any further, the phone on the bureau rang. She got to it first, but when she looked up and saw the worry etched on his battered face, she handed him the receiver.

'Yeah. Yeah, I'm okay man. What dey say?'

Siobhan leaned in and their cheeks touched as she tried to listen with him at the phone.

'They want to transfer him... Oldchurch in Romford. There's a specialist unit there,' Herb said, and then cleared his throat to hide a catch in his voice. 'They said it's touch and go. There's bleeding in his brain and they're worried about damage. I'm going to follow on. I know the way...'

'Herb? You still dere?' Jam asked as the line went quiet.

'Yes. Still here. Look, it's going to be a few hours before we know anything. I'll stay with him. You should get some rest. Er... I know it's not The Ritz, but you can stay at the house as long as you want. Give me your numbers and I'll text you when I know more.'

* * *

Half an hour later, Siobhan unlocked her front door and went inside. It felt cosy and welcoming because the lights and heating were pre-set by timers. The only movement came from the little black cat that stretched up on its white toes and, without looking to acknowledge her arrival, turned and burrowed back into its radiator hammock in a single movement.

'You can come in,' she whispered around the door, and Jam stepped inside with the bag of food. The cat looked up at that point and jumped from his perch to investigate the wonderful smell that had just wafted in with the stranger.

'So, where da baby?' he said in a hushed tone.

'It's okay,' she said, 'you don't have to whisper anymore. Minx... won't tell a soul, as long as you give her some of your fish.'

'I mean what time da childminder bring it back?'

'It's a *her*, not an it,' she scolded, and Jam held up his big hands. 'But you don't have to worry about scaring her with that face. We've got all night.'

'Yeah?'

'No... I mean... she's keeping Eloise all night while Daddy's at work.'

'*Your* daddy?' he said.

'Well, of course. Whose daddy did you think I meant?'

'Da... baby's?'

'Yeah... mine and the baby's... Eloise's daddy.'

'You sisters!'

'Ye-es!' Her eyes rolled with ridicule. 'I thought Jabba was supposed to be the slow one around here.'

'Jokes...' he said, the wheels still grinding painfully in his head. 'An' your mum?'

'Mummy isn't here either,' was all she said, and that didn't help him at all.

'So, we *have* got all night, den.'

'Hey! Before you get too comfortable, mister,' she countered, 'I... will get to have a lie-in tomorrow, and you... you will be going home when I say you're well enough to leave.'

'You know dat.'

'But first,' she said, taking two plates from the cupboard, 'you need to get some of this food inside of you. Then you can have a long soak in the bath.'

'No complaints from us,' he said, kneeling to stroke the cat who was standing with her front paws on the oversized tongue of his Nike trainer, and her tail wrapped around the wrinkled leg of his jeans.

After they ate, Siobhan gave him a towel, underwear and a dressing gown from her father's room, and left him to soak in the bath. The hot water soothed his aches and when he reappeared downstairs, she applied witch hazel to the bruises on his face and settled him on the sofa.

'What music do you like?' she said.

'Garrij,' he said, and when she frowned back, he reeled off a long list of Artful Dodger tracks, few of which she'd heard of.

'How about S Club 7?' she offered with a wry grin and he laughed. 'I know, sorry, Eloise loves them.'

She put on Craig David, went out to the kitchen, and made herself a vodka and orange and brought it in with a glass of water.

'No alcohol for you tonight,' she said, setting down the glasses on the coffee table, and he nodded mournfully.

'No bunnin', neiver?' He cupped his hand to his lips and drew in an exaggerated breath.

'Definitely no marijuana.' She wagged a finger. 'Apart from anything else, Daddy would go ballistic.'

They both laughed.

Before she could sit down, she had to move a pile of children's clothes from the armchair.

'How old is she... Eloise?' Jam asked as he watched her folding one of the dresses.

'Fifteen months,' she replied, and continued smoothing out the fabric.

'She proper lucky havin' a big sister like you.'

'Hmm,' she said, and her eyes lowered. 'They had her very late in life. She wasn't planned.'

'I was finkin' she might be...' he began tentatively, keen to make conversation but increasingly aware of the big question he didn't know how to ask. 'I fought she was yours.'

'She might as well be,' she said, idly taking another garment from the pile and re-folding it.

'Did ya mum... pass away? Jabba's mum almost... when he was born.'

'No, it wasn't the birth. Everything went fine...' She allowed herself a nervous laugh. 'For what they call a geriatric pregnancy.'

'Siobhan?' Jam said and she looked at him. 'You know... Sometime it help to talk... you know, about stuff.'

'We don't know,' she said, exhaling deeply.

'Don't know...?'

'What happened.' She turned and lowered herself slowly into the chair as Jam came across and knelt with her. 'I was living away, down on the coast. Student quarters. Halfway through my last year as a trainee. I would have been qualifying in the summer. She was my inspiration, my mum — a ward sister at King George's.'

Siobhan seemed to perk up, and an ironic smile broke on her lips. 'Thinking about it, she's probably the reason I insisted on coming to check on you and Jabba earlier. She couldn't help caring for people... and that probably rubbed off on me.'

'Have summa dis,' Jam said, picking up her glass, and she took it and sipped the vodka.

'She hadn't long gone back after maternity leave,' she continued strongly, and then her voice trembled. 'I remember the call from Daddy, one morning. He'd just got in from work... She wasn't here. Like, she just *wasn't* here. He'd spoken to her on the phone the night before, same as he always did to say goodnight. She told him she'd just got Eloise off to sleep and was going to have a bath before going to bed. When he got home at eight the next morning, the bath was full but unused, and her nightclothes were still under the pillow. There was no sign of a break-in or a struggle, none of the neighbours saw or heard anything. It was like she'd disappeared in the uniform she'd been wearing all day. When Daddy rushed into the nursery, Eloise was in her cot, cooing and gurgling like nothing had happened.'

'I'm so sorry.' Jam stood and put an arm around her. 'How long... she gone?' Siobhan looked up at him with tears in her eyes.

'Four months, two weeks and one day.'

***

'George?' Ray Riggs' voice was deep and, with a single word, accusatory. He had little patience for George Harris. The man was just the latest in a long line of suckers to think he could buy a top-table seat at the business empire that Riggs had built with his bare hands for over fifteen years.

'Ray. You've heard.' Harris tried to stay calm but he always felt nervous when he had to give Riggs bad news. He also needed to keep his voice down.

'You tell me. Cause I gotta say... I'm not entirely sure I can believe my own... FUCKING EARS.'

'Ray, we got the stuff. It's already gone back out, just like you said... like we wanted. We just ran into a little hitch... at the depot, that's all.'

'You ran into... a little hitch.'

'They were just a couple of kids. Got in the way.'

'Kids? Who were they, George?'

'Er, we... don't know yet.'

'If they were just a couple of kids... what about the lock-up?'

'I sent Ricky back with Geordie to sort them out...'

'How long has Ricky been with us, George? HOW LONG?'

'Couple of years, I s'pose.'

'And Geordie?'

'Longer than me, Ray.'

'And you're telling me a couple of kids... I heard one was just a faggot.'

'It was the other one. He was real 'andy... with his fists. Gave me a few good'uns before I overpowered him.'

'And what about the big powder puff? Did he give you a

68

pasting as well, George... before you overpowered him?'

'I think he was just a bit clumsy, that's all. He went out like a light. Single blow... your boy Tommy took him out.'

'So we have a boxer you went toe to toe with before putting him on the canvas, and a fat nancy with a splitting headache, trussed up in one of my lock-ups. But instead of being dealt with, they get up and walk away, like fucking Lazarus.'

'They couldn't have... taken out Ricky and Geordie, not in the state they were in. They must have had help.'

'I want you to bring them here, George... our lads. I want to know what happened.'

'That's the problem, Ray.'

'There's only one problem, from where I'm sitting. You were in charge of this and the two kids escaped under your nose. So tell me what the other problem is.'

'Ricky and Geordie... it's like they just disappeared. I even went there myself. They're gone.'

'I'm going to pretend I didn't hear that, George. And I'm going to keep pretending for the next forty-eight hours.'

'We don't know what happened to them.'

'George?'

'Yes, Ray.'

'You still want an equal slice of the action, yeah?'

'Yeah, Ray. I'm all in, you know I am. We're partners, right...'

'George?'

'Yes, Ray.'

'Forty-eight hours.'

'For what?'

'I want two bodies. And if you can't give me Ricky and Geordie, you'd better make sure it's those two youngsters that got in the way. And if it ain't any of them bodies... George, I'll settle for just one. And you know I mean it.'

'But Ray...'

'Forty-eight hours, George. Clock's ticking.'

George Harris exhaled deeply and tossed the phone down.

The woman lying on the bed didn't flinch but continued staring at the ceiling. Harris walked around to her, took a tissue from the bedside cabinet and wiped the saliva that had started to run from the corner of her mouth.

'You know I'm doing this for you, Tracy,' he said, and swept the hair from her eyes, letting the back of his hand rest for a second on her cheek, before leaning to kiss her forehead. He picked up the phone and left the room.

Without the usual pause to chat with the staff—there were only so many times he could hear them tell him not to give up hope—he left the private clinic and selected a number on his phone as he walked to the car.

'Tommy,' he said, when the call was answered. 'Your old man's being a diva. You concentrate on tracking down Ricky and Geordie and I'll see what I can do about the other two.'

'Alright, George. I'm on it.' Tommy Riggs was also feeling nervous. But he knew his old man would always side with him if things got out of hand. He was more concerned with what was still *in* the lock-up. 'What about the consignment? I *said* we shouldn't have taken them there.'

'It's okay. I went back and checked. Some of the crates had been moved but they're all still there and none have been opened. We'll go back tomorrow and move it all, yeah?'

'Sure. I just don't want Dad finding out... you know... that we've gone behind his back.'

'Keep your cool, Tom. This is just between you and me.'

'Well... the money he expects me to live on... it's pitiful.'

'Nothing's going to go wrong. And remember, I need that extra money more than you do.'

7.

Jam woke with a jolt and grabbed at his head. In a few seconds, the pain eased and he repositioned the pillow and tried to get comfortable. The movement was enough to wake Siobhan, who was dozing lightly in the armchair. After he'd comforted her, she insisted he should get some sleep on the sofa and she watch him for a while until he nodded off. Then she'd brought her own pillow and duvet down from her room and covered him over.

'What time is it?' he mumbled.

'Just after one. How are you feeling?'

'Got a headache, for real.'

'I'll get you something,' she said, and went to the kitchen.

She hadn't really thought this through, beyond him getting some sleep, and now realised the house was cold and she no longer had a made-up bed of her own to go to. When she came back in with the painkiller, she could see he wasn't comfortable, and it probably wasn't helping his battered body to be curled up like that. She gently stroked his hair and his swollen eyes opened.

'You probably need to lay flat,' she said, and he winced as he lifted himself up on his elbows.

'Maybe da floor is better,' he said, and slowly swung his legs round.

'I've got another idea,' she said, and helped him to his feet. She wrapped the duvet around both their shoulders and guided him towards the stairs.

'Let's get you into bed,' she said, once they were in her room.

'You're da nurse,' he said with a tired smile.

'And you'll do as you're told,' she said, untying the belt and opening the dressing gown.

He groaned as he lowered his arms.

'Oh my God!' she said, when she saw the bruises around his ribs. 'Sit back on the bed and I'll put some more witch hazel on.'

***

Terry Pinner was about to leave for home when the unregistered mobile vibrated in his pocket.

'What time do you call this, George?' he whispered, with a furtive glance around the subdued office. He could only see one or two officers hunched behind computer screens at the far end, but decided nonetheless to slip out through the fire exit into the stairwell.

'Sorry, Tel. We've got a problem.'

'I thought you said it all went fine.'

'It did... It was. But now there's a loose end. Someone knew about the switch and there was a bit of action at the depot.'

'You are kidding me, George.'

'I wish I was, but this is deadly serious.'

'Jesus, this is my friggin' job we're talking about here.'

'I know, Tel. We thought we'd dealt with it, but...'

'But what?'

'They got away.'

'Oh great! There's me thinking you lot handled these kinds of problems all the time. I'd rather not know the details, but how the hell did that happen?'

'We don't really know. They had help. And now two of our boys are missing.'

'Well, that sounds more like your problem than mine.'

'Yeah, but Ray wanted me to ask you personally if you can help track down the outsiders. One of them's in a bad way. Head injury. Trouble is, we don't know how they got out or where they ended up.'

'Right, let me get this straight. It's gone ten o'clock – and I was just heading home to my wife and those *lovely* kids by the way – and you want me to find a couple of guys somewhere in London because you let them get away. Now, how the hell am I supposed to do that?'

'You must have ways of finding out hospital admissions in suspicious circumstances, don't you?'

'And you think that's going to be easy?'

'Tel, do what you can, yeah. Ray will… I mean, Ray and *me*… will be very grateful. Help us with this and I'll make sure you're back at the top table.'

'I'll make some calls, but I'm not promising anything, George. This is a hunt for a needle in a stack of sodding needles.'

***

Deep down, somewhere in his soul, Raymond Riggs loved his wife, Natalie. But Jesus Christ, she did annoy him sometimes. Not that it was usually her fault that he was angry. Most of the time, he had those morons who worked for him to blame for that. But wasn't she supposed to be there to relieve his stress and take the problems of the day away? Wasn't that why he let her spend so much of his fucking money?

He watched her walk into the bedroom, in those expensive silk pyjamas. His own money spent on something designed to deny him the sight of even an inch of his own wife's body. And when she got into the satin sheets, without even acknowledging his presence, she put on those hideous laced eyeshades before turning away from him and switching off her lamp. Were they to deny him looking at her face? Or were they so she didn't have to see him?

It had been a pleasant enough evening… considering. She'd made a hearty meal. Maybe that's what he actually loved about her. At least she could cook. And she kept the house nice. But surely anyone could do that. There was supposed to be more. She was supposed to do more. For him. What a life she had. Everything on a silver tray, but what did he get in return? Pyjamas and a face mask.

He reached across and pulled at the elastic around her head and she froze rigid. He held it taut until it dug into the grooves of his fingers and she grabbed at the lace to prevent it cutting into her eyes. When he let it go, she let out a muffled cry and braced herself for what was coming next.

***

It was gone three and Siobhan's hopes of a good night's sleep and a blissful lie-in were a distant memory. In nothing but the tight-fitting stripy trunks she had found for him in her dad's drawer, Jam had crashed within seconds of lying back on her bed. She had managed to squeeze in behind him and wrestle some of the duvet over her shoulder, but otherwise, she took what warmth she could get from his body heat.

His swollen nose slowed his breathing to a laboured rasp and his sleep had been disturbed by frequent bouts of violent dreaming that at one point was so bad, she had to wake him from it for her own safety. She had watched the hands on her bedside clock move slowly around the dial and in less than two hours, the alarm she'd forgotten to reset would ring.

She reached over his chest to grab the clock so she could move the small silver hand on by another half an hour, but he turned onto his side and she lost her grip on it. When it hit the floor with a thud, he bolted upright and the calming hand she placed on his shoulder made him turn quickly, fists clenched.

'It's only me,' she said with a gentle smile. The swelling had eased under his eye and a hint of the cheeky, handsome guy who had tried hitting on her two days ago was beginning to return. However, the bruising was now starting to take on shades of green, but in the early morning gloom, she had to admit, he was looking good again. 'How are you feeling, Sleeping Beauty?'

'Don't you have to kiss me,' he whispered through a boyish grin, 'to wake me up?'

'We'll have to see what Nurse Siobhan says about that,' she said.

***

Riggs limped from the bedroom, pawing at the scar on his forehead. It always seemed to bother him at times of heightened stress. But now it was also bleeding, because earlier she had caught it with those five grands' worth of diamonds on her hand, when she'd managed to free her left arm and swing it back in his face. The engagement ring he had bought for her. Again, she had used his own money against him. Bitch.

He hobbled down the stairs and tripped on the bottom step, initially cursing the leg that hadn't functioned properly for so many years, but then he let out a deep, hideous laugh.

'At least I can get down the FUCKING STAIRS!' he screamed into the darkness. 'She won't be walking anywhere soon.'

Lifeless eyes stared at the bedroom wall. Her conscious mind was elsewhere, detached from the person lying face-down on the sullied sheets. A place where no frayed remnants of silk could dig deep into her wrists and ankles. Where blood couldn't seep from her ruptured anus. Somewhere she couldn't feel the pain; where numbness was her only comfort. A refuge from the reality too awful to accept.

Downstairs, he turned on the TV and increased the volume to drown out the noises in his head. He'd give it an hour for her to learn her lesson. Then he'd make her camomile tea and run her a hot bath.

***

Siobhan gave her patient a small kiss on the lips and Jam raised his arms in an attempt to take her head in his hands. But when the pain in his ribs made him stop halfway, she pulled back.

'That's all for now,' she said, and his mouth slumped.

'But...'

'You can't even move,' she said, before noticing the skimpy shorts were failing to conceal, much less constrain his enthusiasm. 'Apart from... that!'

'Yeah,' he grinned, awkwardly. 'I fink ev'ryfink's still workin' down dere.'

To his surprise and sheer delight, she reached for his waistband and lowered it, so that before he could react, she held his growing erection in her hand.

'Ah!' he exclaimed.

'Ah, indeed,' she said, watching it judder rhythmically before curling her hand around it.

'So,' he said, his breath now coming in shallow waves. 'Is dis a... medical procedure?'

'Hmm,' she said, wistfully. 'Matron has decided to give you a fuller examination after all, seeing as you're now... up and about.'

He laughed and then put his hand gently on her arm. 'Is cool wiv me, baby, but you sure you wanna do dis?'

She paused and smiled back at him. 'Maybe we both need this,' she said, and he lowered himself back onto the pillow and closed his eyes.

Her touch was firm and then fleeting, and he had to empty his mind for fear of embarrassing himself. But she seemed to know just when to stop. And when she did, he would lie there waiting for her to start again. Then, after a while, when she stopped and didn't resume, he opened his eyes. Her hands were no longer on him because they were over her head, removing the camisole top she had worn to bed. He feasted his eyes on her small, pale breasts with their dark, rigid points that stood outward as she reached up, before regaining their fullness when she lowered her arms. And when she saw him looking, she leaned forward inviting him to reach them with his mouth.

Then she was standing, just long enough to loosen the bow on her cami-knickers and let them fall to the floor. Her lustrous hair lay around her shoulders like a silken shawl and some part of him wanted her to stand there longer, but she wasted no time climbing onto him. Now she kissed him properly, being careful not to press her face against his tender nose and eyes. He took her tongue into his mouth, hungrily, and rolled it around with his own. He could feel her hands on him again and he had to look up and study the pattern on the ceiling to keep from losing it too soon. She was reaching into a drawer and unwrapping a condom, and her grip became firmer as she put it on him.

'You're proper buff, baby,' he whispered.

'Whatever that means...' she said, smiling up at him, 'it must be nice.'

'You know dat,' he said.

Her hands now came back up to his face and she gently brushed his cheek before resting her palms on the pillow either side of his head and easing herself forward. She took him inside her and he buried his face in her neck. She eased down, slowly, exhaling in a rhythmic groan as she felt his full size touch her deeper than she had known before. And when she lifted forward, she arched her back so he could feast on her breasts again. The next time she slid down, he thrust forward and she thought she would explode. She held him within her longer and then slowly released again. And each time she lifted, he groaned and suckled her breasts. And each time she lowered, he closed his eyes and leaned back into the pillow. They both forgot the pain in his ribs. She could tell he was holding on, desperate not to let it go, but she pressed down again, this time reaching back with her arms and gripping under his hips to pull him further in. The change of movement tweaked her just as he was at his peak and this time she didn't release him and he was left to work alone, clenching and withdrawing, thrusting and easing... until they both cried out and colours shuddered through her head and his brain exploded in a million bursts of light.

8.

Thursday

By six o'clock, Siobhan and Jam were walking to the café. It didn't open until six-thirty but she said if they were early, she could probably persuade Brian to let him come in and have the first of the day's bacon and eggs. As they walked away from the house, Jam reached for her hand, but she gently slid it out of his grasp and lightly rubbed the side of his arm instead. He tried not to be bothered by it and supposed she didn't want any of her neighbours to see them acting like she was his girl. Either that or the thought of holding hands with a man dressed in her father's old shirt, jumper, jeans and jacket was a place she wasn't willing to go yet.

Although the clothes were a good fit, Jam had never felt so uncomfortable. The crotch in the jeans left no room for manoeuvre and the labels were all wrong. In the absence of a hood, he tried to make the best of it by raising the collar on the leather jacket. But the balled-up, day-old socks he'd stuffed behind the tongues of his Nike creps just seemed to exaggerate the swing of his hips with every awkward step.

'Do you think you can handle a full English this early in the morning?' Siobhan said, diverting his attention.

'Not normally,' he said. 'But dis ain't ma normal kinda mornin'.'

'Oh, okay,' she said, and smiled back at him. 'Given you an appetite, have I?'

'I'm proper starvin',' he said, and they laughed together as they turned into the next street.

A cold wind whipped around the corner and Siobhan was

grateful for the trousers she'd opted for today. The same gust had a sobering effect on Jam's mood and he instantly felt guilty for enjoying himself so much, with Jabba in hospital and no idea how he was doing.

'I never got no message from Herb, did you?'

'Nothing,' she said. 'Couldn't you call *him*?'

'I bell him, yeah. You was in da shower. But, like da man say, da number don't work.'

'What about the hospital?'

'Oh yeah, man. Oldchurch, huh. Wha'gwun dere? Dey say dey can't find him.'

'They what?'

'I tell dem his real name, but dey say he not dere.'

'Oh, that's ridiculous. There must be a misunderstanding.'

'Yeah, baby. Gonna sort dem out later.' He shook his head and they walked the rest of the way in silence.

Ten minutes later, he followed her through the side door that led towards the staffroom behind the café. The heat coming from the kitchen made his cold fingers tingle as he edged along the narrow corridor, stacked high with white plastic trays of fresh bread, pastries and cakes. He could smell hot oil and hear bacon and sausages sizzling under a grill. Through a door-less entrance on the right, amid the steam and industrialised din of low-end cuisine, a middle-aged man and a younger woman in matching clean blue aprons juggled a dozen different pots and pans with the speed and coordination of street dancers. When they reached the small room at the end of the passageway, Jam stood and watched as Siobhan removed her coat and took a fresh apron from the box on a chair and put the loop over her head.

'Still alive then?' It was an unfamiliar accent, its tone sardonic, but the voice behind him was unthreatening and Jam spun around to see who was asking. He recognised the café owner, standing at the door, with a look of abject horror in his eyes. He was average height and build, and although his hair was silver-grey, Jam guessed he was in his mid-thirties. Jam could only shrug and wait for the man to explain himself.

'Sorry, Brian,' Siobhan cut in. 'I completely forgot. We...' She looked at Jam. 'It got a bit tense.'

'Yeah... crikey, I can see that,' he said, as he continued staring at Jam's face. 'And that's what I was afraid of.'

'No, not like that. I was fine. It was Jam... and his friend. He's in hospital.'

'And Mr Angry?'

'Yeah, he was... just a bit... strange. But no, nothing to worry about. Look, Brian, I was hoping we could give Jam something to eat before he goes to see Jabba.'

'Sorry to hear about your mate... Jim,' he said, and put his hand on Jam's arm. 'I hope he's okay.'

'Yeah man... s'Jam.'

'No worries. Before you start, love...' He turned to Siobhan, 'go into the kitchen and get them to plate up the special. He can eat out there, if he likes, while you help me unpack the baked goods.'

'Fanks cuz,' Jam said. 'How much...'

'On the house, Jam. Just let us know how your friend is.' With that, he turned and took three trays from the top of the stack and carried them through to the counter.

Siobhan left Jam in the kitchen, holding a plate that was being piled high. When she followed Brian into the serving area with the last two bakery trays, he turned and grinned at her.

'What?' she said, and started to blush.

'No lie-in for you this morning then?'

'I could hardly send him home in the middle of the night after the beating he got, could I?' she said, poker-faced, and turned away to lift cakes from the tray.

He leaned closer to whisper in her ear. 'Looks like he's not the only one who got a good spanking.'

'Brian!' she spluttered, her face now red.

'He's a good-looking boy though... under all those bruises. And very fit.'

'Keep your eyes off... and your hands to yourself, Brian. I

saw him first. He's mine!'

They both laughed as Jam came through with his breakfast, smiling across at them without really knowing why.

***

Jam arrived at Oldchurch Hospital just before nine. There would be no point getting there any earlier, Siobhan had told him when she'd given him the bus routes; the first to Gants Hill and the second on to Romford.

He'd said goodbye and left the café, trying not to feel disappointed that she'd simply squeezed his hand and offered him her last cigarette when he'd leaned in for a kiss. So, with time to kill, he'd lit it up, pulled up his collar and walked around the block past the strange house with the new storage rooms. It was as deserted as they'd left it the night before, and he continued walking a loop that would take him to the bus stop.

The traffic was heavy and cars were pulling away from their overnight parking slots along the roads, but he saw no sign of the white van or of Herb's Mercedes. By the time he'd finally jostled with commuters on the 179, he'd forgotten about his face, but few of them looked at him and quickly turned away.

At the reception desk, he waited for the woman to finish her phone call and when she peered up at him, she barely acknowledged his appearance, even though the bruises now merged around his eyes like tie-dyed circles.

'I phone before, yeah. My bruvver come in las night an' I need to see him... Please.'

'Visiting hours start at 10.30. You'll have to wait until then.'

'Can you tell me how he is? He ain't got no family...'

'I can phone the ward sister if you can tell me where he is.'

'Dunno. You say... before... *you* dunno. He mus' be here, somewhere. All I know is he's gonna have a operation... on his head. It was proper bruck up. I don't even know if he...'

'What name?'

'Er... Jabba.'

82

'Don't tell me...' she said, shaking her head. 'Mr Wocky, I suppose. Security!'

'Nah... you don't get me. His real name... 's'Milton Graham... but like I say on da phone, yeah, da person wiv him don't know dat.'

'Just a second,' she said, waving away the man with the logo on his epaulettes who was sauntering over, and tapped the keyboard in front of her. 'No. The only Grahams we have are a lady in the maternity unit and a long-stay in Elderly Care.'

'But I don't fink it'll say Graham,' he said, and she looked back at him bewildered. A middle-aged couple who were now standing behind him tut-tutted to each other.

'And you're sure it was this hospital?' she said, and he nodded back. 'Okay, I'll try one more thing and then I'm going to have to ask you to wait while I help some of these other people.'

He could sense there were now several behind him but he didn't want to turn around and scare them.

'Right,' she continued. 'Did he arrive by ambulance or was he a walk-in?'

'It musta been a ambulance.'

'Must it?' she said with a sigh. 'And what time was he admitted?'

'It was in da evenin', sumfink after seven.'

'So you don't really know when either?'

'He come here from Whipps Cross. You brung him here, yeah. How do I know when he get here, man?'

'Okay!' she countered. 'Who was with him? Sometimes we log the carer if the patient is...'

'Yeah, he wouldna bin conscious. But I only know da man wiv him as Herb.'

'And you don't know *his* surname?' she said, dropping her hands in exasperation. 'This is useless. Please step aside and let me...'

'Look, I dunno his surname, but *he* would only know ma bruvver's name as Jabba.'

'Highly unlikely,' she said beginning to type again. 'J-A...'

'Double-B, A.'

'Well I never,' she said. 'Must be him. Neurology. Says here his surname is Anglich. Mean anything?'

'Nah,' he said.

'Well, this is highly irregular,' she said, looking over her spectacles at him. 'What is your name?'

'Ja... Michaels,' he said. 'Kingston Michaels.'

'But you said he was your brother.'

'Innit dough. Ma bredren.' The receptionist rolled her eyes.

'Alright, Mr Michaels,' she said, writing it on her notepad. 'I'll make a call and see what I can find out.'

'Fank you.'

'If he's in ICU, they might let you see him. If not, you'll have to wait until visiting time. Now take a seat.' When he turned away, the queue behind him didn't seem as long after all.

Terry Pinner sat at the end of the second row, held up his newspaper and re-crossed his legs, as the young man with the badly-bruised face came and sat directly in front of him. He lowered the paper enough to peer over the young man's shoulder and watched as he took out his mobile, selected a contact and pushed the green button.

"S'Jam,' the young man said. 'I fink we found him. Yeah, in da Neuro-sumfink place. So he's still... you know. Yeah, you know dat... Nah, haven't seen him yet. Waitin' for someone to find out when. Herb? Nah. He's not at da house or here. Did he tell you his surname...? Sumfink like Anglican? Nah? Dunno what dey chattin' den. Anyway, wha'gwun dere...? For real. I'll bell you later, yeah... after I see him. Might not be till dis afternoon; you know what dey like in hospital... Yeah, for real. Laters.'

The young man ended the call, keeping the woman's name visible on the screen, and Pinner turned back to his crossword. Within the grid, he had already written 'Anglich' across the bottom and added 'Milton Graham' at three down, intersecting with the lower 'A'. With 'Kingston Michaels' now at five down, in a perfect alignment across the top, he wrote 'Siobhan Jennings'.

84

Finally, he scrawled a thick black circle several times around the name 'Anglich', folded the paper and got up to walk away.

After a few hesitant seconds waiting for the lift doors to close, Jam decided he'd rather take the stairs. He wasn't ready to be closed in a confined space just yet. After almost half an hour, he was dozing in the chair when the woman on reception had called his name across the waiting room and told him someone would see him on the second floor, first door on the right.

At the top of the stairs, he saw the directions to ICU pointing left, whereas all the doors to the right were marked: 'Strictly Staff Only'. He went left and a woman with a stethoscope around her neck walked towards him. She smiled and asked him where he was going.

'First door on da right.'

'Ah, yes. You must be Mr Michaels.'

'Yeah, I've come to see Jabba.'

'Yes, Mr Anglich... isn't it,' she said, and he nodded rather than correct her. 'He's very poorly, I'm afraid. Why don't we go through here?' She led him into a small room awash with the early spring sun that shone in sideways like a torch-beam. She offered him a seat at a clinical white, laminated table and adjusted the vertical blinds to reduce the glare in his eyes. 'I'll go and get the notes,' she said, and left him alone.

The words 'very poorly' hung in the air like a dark cloud in a blue sky; hearing them from a medical person had made them sound even worse. Doctors and nurses always spoke in riddles, like they were trying to make things seem better than they were and at the same time, telling you stuff you didn't want to hear.

He didn't think it was odd when there was a knock at the door. Although he instinctively responded, it was unnecessary, as a man wearing a suit had already entered.

'Mr Michaels, don't get up,' he said, but Jam was on his feet. 'Please... take a seat. This won't take a moment.'

Jam remained standing until the man had walked to the other side of the table, pulled out the chair and sat down opposite him. Jam had seen enough on the telly to know a man in a suit was always someone senior. This one was probably a brain surgeon, and when the man removed something from his inside pocket and slid it across the table, he braced himself for the worst.

'Detective Constable James Melville, sir, Metropolitan Police.' Jam's hackles instantly rose when he saw the badge.

'What?' Jam's eyes narrowed and he slumped back in the chair.

'I'd just like to ask you a few questions, sir,' the policeman said, taking back the warrant card. 'Like I said, it won't take long.'

'I only come to see ma bruvver.'

'It's okay, sir. I know this must be distressing for you, but when someone is admitted to hospital and their injuries are, let's say a little extreme...' He was staring at Jam's face but not looking from his mouth to his eyes in a conversational way. He was staring at the bruises, and for a moment, Jam thought he was talking about *his* injuries.

'What me? Nah. Dis was jus' a bus' up in da pub.'

'Well, now you come to mention it, sir, that is a pretty nasty beating you've taken there. Has this... attack been reported?'

'Look, man, I didn't come here to talk about me. I want someone to start tellin' me about Jab.'

'Okay. That's fair enough, sir. I was actually talking about the injuries sustained by your friend. Whipps Cross alerted us last night, because they didn't think the story stacked up and, frankly, they were a little suspicious of the person who had brought him in. So, do you know how he was hurt? Perhaps it was something to do with this... altercation, in a pub?'

'Nah, man. Dat was a accident. One of da doors. Proper heavy dey is. He's helpin' me fit dem. I fink da top is screwed in. Den it drop... on him.'

'And his name is... Jab?'

'Jabba.'

'But the man who brought him here last night said his surname was Anglich. Does that name mean anything to you?'

'Nah.'

'And the man who brought him in, he's your guv'nor, is he?'

'Nah.'

'Okay. What can you tell me about him?'

'Nuffink.'

'Do you know his name?'

'Nah.'

'Well it seems he followed the ambulance here but left after the operation and no one now seems to know who he was. Is it possible *his* name is Anglich? It's just that we're trying to understand where that name comes from.'

'All I know is ma bruvver's called Jabba. His real name is Milton Graham, yeah? He hasn't got no one else.'

'No other next of kin?'

'It was jus' him and his mum, but she die. Now can I go see him, man? Dis is proper liber'ies.'

'Okay, I'll ask the doctor if you can go through, but if I do, you have to agree to come back in here afterwards and my colleague will take a full statement. Will you do that... if I talk to the doctor?'

'For real. I jus' wanna talk to him. Hear his voice.'

'We're... er, waiting to hear what he has to say, as well... Uh, I'm sure the doctor will give you all the details.'

'Wha'jer mean?' Jam said in alarm.

'You really don't know, do you?' he said, and for the first time since he walked in, he looked genuinely concerned.

'What?'

'I'm sorry, sir. But your friend is in a deep coma.'

Pinner was taking a risk just being there, so far from his own turf. He knew there were police on the second floor. And to make matters worse, he already knew Melville. Knew a hell of a lot more about the detective constable than the officer knew about him. But, the fact he was known to Melville was a big problem – they would recognise each other in the street. Like they had once before.

That day two men had died. The Notting Hill Carnival had a habit of dividing some people while bringing others together. Today, he just wanted to keep tabs on the young guy. He couldn't afford to be seen by the Met. Not here. And not now.

9.

On seeing Jabba, his head heavily bandaged and an array of tubes and pipes coming from his nose, mouth and arms, Jam was in a state of shock. The little, fat boy he'd decided to protect all those years ago, and had done so ever since, was lying there lifeless. But without a visible mark on his body, it was hard to accept he'd been hurt at all. The number of times Jam had seen him bruised, bloodied and humiliated. Yet now, he looked somehow untouchable, peaceful and serene. And the reason he was there, closer to death than anyone would ever want to be, was because, for once in his life, Jabba had been coming to help *him*. The one time that Jam hadn't been able to protect him.

Jam held his friend's dimpled hand until the consultant arrived to speak with him. Much of what she said didn't sink in. They had been able to stop the bleeding into the brain, but words like subarachnoid haemorrhage, intracranial hypertension and neurological impairment didn't mean a thing to him. He understood percentages though and soon realised Jabba was, in fact, very lucky to be alive. When he asked when his friend would wake up, the doctor looked down as she replied.

'It's impossible to say at this stage.' She shook her head, sagely. 'We will artificially maintain his unconscious state to give his brain the best chance to heal. We won't know what lasting damage there may have been for days, possibly weeks. But the next 48 hours are critical. After that, we'll have a better idea.'

Jam returned to the bright, little family room in a haze of remorse. The WPC who was waiting for him spoke kindly and brought him some tea. When she had finished writing down everything he said, he looked down at the form with the pen in his hand. The weight of responsibility for Jabba's condition was unbearable. But worse than that was the sense of betrayal, as he signed the page, knowing it was all a pack of lies.

When he walked away from the hospital, the tears he'd shed when finally left alone in that small, sunlit room had dried. Now, there was nothing more he could do for his friend to make him better. But there was a lot he could do to make things right.

As he called Siobhan to give her the news, he didn't notice the man in the dark suit watching him leave.

***

Herb Long was driving back from the Clacket Lane services on the M25. It had been a fruitful meeting. The unofficial representative of a large Chinese manufacturer was keen to update him about the container on-board a ship, currently somewhere in the Mediterranean. With the paperwork having gone missing, the rep had been instructed to make discreet enquiries with several favoured distributors. The question he had for Herb was: could he absorb two thousand handbags, each with a retail value of £600 into his network and drip-feed them into the UK market over the following six months? With the new storage facilities in South Woodford now ready, and the increased capacity from the Gravesend losses still not fully taken up, he'd been able to give reassurances that he was well-positioned for the deal.

Now, he was in a hurry to get back to Gravesend before the latest consignment of near-perfect, branded sportswear ended its long journey from Mauritius at the inconspicuous residential property he still called home. But there was something else on his mind. Mac had called earlier to let him know he'd dealt with things at Chatham. Herb knew precisely what that meant and consequently began to harbour serious concerns for Jam and Siobhan's safety.

He pulled up at traffic lights and took out his phone, selected the number he'd stored yesterday and waited for it to connect. When it went to an answer machine, he raised his eyebrows as the slightly muffled recording began to play. He barely knew the song, but recognised its opening line.

'Tank fly boss walk jam nitty gritty, you're listening to the boy from the big bad city, this is Jam Hot, this is Jam Hot.'

'Jam, right...' he said, with a shake of his head after the rap had ended abruptly with a beep. 'This is Herb. Uh... call me back on this number. There's something you need to know.'

**

That had been a close call. When Kingston Michaels had appeared from the stairwell and headed for the exit, the last thing Pinner had expected as he rushed to keep up was for the lift doors to open ahead and for Melville to walk right out in front of him. If the detective constable had turned at that moment, the newly-promoted Detective Inspector Terence Pinner would have had a lot of explaining to do. Instead, he'd been able to use his momentum to veer off into the empty lift. Luckily, no one else got in. He held the lift until he could see the policeman walk out the main exit and then he stepped back out into the corridor without drawing any attention.

Once he'd caught up with the young man at the bus stop, he was able to stay with him all the way to Dagenham. And when he saw him buy a ticket at the machine, he decided he had to take the chance. He needed to find out more about this guy. But rather that his name and several others he'd never heard of before, it was Anglich that had stood out like neon. When he saw it on the text message earlier that morning from the techie he'd unofficially instructed to trawl suspicious admissions through the night, he knew he was onto something.

Maintaining his distance, he went up and spoke to the attendant at the barrier who let him through without a word. Once he set eyes on his target again on the westbound platform, he slipped back out of sight. He had no idea where this was going to lead, but he'd already turned his phone off so no one could reach him.

The train pulled in and he got on the last carriage and made his way to the end so he could see through to the next one. The young guy had a seat and stared mindlessly at the undulating blur of blackness as the train rattled through the tunnels.

It was a long, tedious journey into central London on the District Line, and he kept checking to make sure Kingston Michaels didn't get off, until he noticed after a few stops that the lad had fallen asleep. By the time they reached Victoria and boarded a train destined for Dover Priory, he was pretty sure where they were heading.

Apart from the prospect of another hour on a train, it couldn't have been a better outcome if he'd planned the route himself. At least once he was there, he could be himself again. And there was every chance he'd be back in the office by mid-afternoon. That was assuming he could get one of his lackeys – and he already someone in mind – to come and get him. Better still, he'd drop her at a station so she could go up north and bring back his car.

***

When Mac had rescued them from the lock-up, apart from ranting on about having wrecked the wrong door trying to find them, he had half-carried Jabba to the van parked out of sight a few hundred yards away. Jam had followed him, trying to memorise the area, and once they'd emerged from the narrow lane out onto the main road, he'd noticed, as they drove past, the train station sign said Rainham. Whilst he was more familiar with its namesake in Essex, he at least now knew of the small town on the Medway estuary, south of Chatham.

He exited the train station and turned left as his phone pinged with the sound of a new text. When he looked, he also found he'd missed a call from a number he didn't recognise. He called voicemail and listened to Herb's brief message, but when he called the number back, it went unanswered. He didn't like the way Herb had made the words 'something you need to know' sound so worrying, but what could he do? He'd try again later.

After another left turn, he came to the entrance to the lane that he knew would take him back to the lock-ups. Before crossing the road, he looked around. It wasn't that he sensed anything wrong; he just wanted to be sure no one was watching. Apart from the free-flowing traffic at that time of day, he could see an old lady looking into a shop window, and someone who looked like an estate agent staring up at a house's roof and writing something on a piece of paper. He walked quickly down the gravel track.

Now he was here, finding the right row of identical garage doors was going to be harder than he'd thought. Those first few minutes outside the lock-up had been almost surreal. He'd had to fight for his life and then watch as a man he'd winded only the day before not only turn up out of nowhere to save them and fight off his attackers, but then proceed to snap their necks like they were cockerels caught in the henhouse. As the memories played out as clear as a DVD in his head, he looked from row to row, searching for some other recognisable feature. He thought he would find a door, if not busted open, at least visibly damaged, but nothing looked out of place.

After pacing back and forth along row after row, he noticed something odd. One of the doors had a ripple along its bottom edge, and he knelt down for a better look. Now he was closer, he could see that the damage was only superficial and it didn't look like the door had actually been opened from that point.

Then he noticed a dip in the gravel next to his knee. Some of the sharp edges of the stones were sticky and red. Maybe this *was* it, he thought, and looked around. That's when he saw the crowbar on the ground, almost hidden in the shade. But not only was the gravel path shaded from the sun, when he looked up at the door, the entire block sat in the shadow of a large industrial unit that ran along this side of the boundary.

That was it, he thought; the sun had been in his eyes when the door had opened. He just needed to find a set of doors in the full glare of the early afternoon sun. He grabbed the bar and retraced his steps along the path, one row at a time. The shadow cast on each set of doors fell lower and lower until he reached the very last row, where the doors were all completely lit by sunshine.

He walked confidently to the middle of the row, and straight to the door he was convinced must have been the one. When he saw the heavy locks at each of the four fixtures, he exhaled deeply.

With no way of knowing whether the outside of the door had been secured this way, he had to assume someone had been back and locked it. He sat there with the warmth radiating on his back and thought about heading home. He felt ready to climb into his own bed and join his friend in an induced coma, in the hope that when they both finally woke up, everything was back to the way it was.

He was about to turn and head back to the central path when a final memory of the previous day dropped into his mind. With Jabba leaning against the side wall, he had put all that wasted effort into moving crates so he could get to the source of daylight. And when he finally got there, all he could see was another row of these ugly garage doors. So, they couldn't have been in this end row. Any windows in the backs of these would look straight onto the boundary fence and the estuary beyond.

When he reached the central path and turned right to go down the next row, something made him stop dead in his tracks. His footfalls in the gravel stopped but the sound of crunching stones repeated like an echo behind him. But when he spun around, there was no one there. Tightening his grip on the crowbar, he stood with his feet planted firmly in the divots they had drilled into the shingle.

Ten, maybe twenty seconds passed without him moving. Silence. He must have imagined it. As quietly as he could, he stepped lightly towards the middle door, and that's when he saw the puddle on the ground. It had a dark, reflective surface, but when his foot rolled a large stone into it, a coloured sludge stirred up from below, turned it a cloudy maroon.

He looked up at the door. All its padlocks were open. Glancing around furtively, he grabbed the handle. It squealed loudly as he lifted it and the sun poured in. He wasn't really expecting to find the bodies and so it was no surprise when all that was left was a sticky pool of black blood, slowly soaking into the concrete. There was no sign of the heavy chain either, but again, ghoulish curiosity wasn't what had brought him back. As a southpaw, he had boxed on the offensive, always taking the fight to his opponent. Defence was never part of his strategy and he wasn't about to start now. He took the crowbar and started jemmying the lids off the wooden crates.

He's got balls, this one. Pinner admired the young man's nerve. In broad daylight, as well. There he was, breaking open crates in a lock-up on a private site, notoriously known to be rented out to some of the most hardened criminals currently not reclining at Her Majesty's pleasure. And no doubt quite a few others who were.

The question was, should he break cover and intervene? If he did so in an official capacity, he'd have to take the lad in, and that would raise a whole boatload of awkward questions. But he could hardly just walk in on him and expect to have a quiet chat. He wondered what George would want him to do. Maybe that was all he could do, and he took out his phone and composed a text.

Jam didn't know what to make of it. Two crates opened and among the coarse wood shavings, all he'd found were metal castings, heavily-greased cogs and precision-turned spindles. Each layer he revealed, as he scooped armfuls of wood chips onto the floor, included larger and heavier pieces than the previous one, but without any obvious markings and no diagrams in the crates, he had no idea what they were or if and how any of them would fit together.

The ones he could lift, he placed, one by one, onto the floor like he was emptying a giant's 3D compendium of machine-engineered jigsaw pieces. But it was pointless to go any further. He'd have to empty them all to have any hope of pairing any of them up. And what would that prove anyway? Apart from anything else, there wasn't going to be room on the floor to unpack many more. But, he figured, while he was here, he may as well open as many crates as he could to be sure they were all of a similar ilk.

There was a lot of noise coming from the lock-up but from where Pinner was hiding, he couldn't see what the guy was discovering. He hoped it was only Taiwanese unlicensed replica car parts or reject solar panels exported surreptitiously by corrupt Chinese disposal agents. He knew Riggs' business interests were diverse and, most of it, he was sure was entirely legitimate. But on the illicit side, he preferred not to think about how far the man would go to turn a profit.

The text reply came back almost instantly: 'Keep him there. On our way.' Pinner turned his phone off, took out his North Kent CID warrant card, and approached the open door.

Jam tried to lift another crate down but it was too heavy and he had to push hard against it to even get it to slide across the top of the one it was sitting on. He pushed it further than he meant and it started to tip forward. When he tried to hold it back, he lost his footing and it fell. As it did so, the figure of a man in a dark suit came into view outside. The estate agent from earlier, he thought. But by then, the crate had crashed to the ground onto its side, and the wooden slats of its lid snapped like twigs under the weight of the object that had broken through.

It caught the suit by surprise and he had to jump back to avoid it as it rolled out towards him. Jam needed no further prompting to make his move and he was out in the sunshine and running before the man could react. At the central path, he turned towards the exit and continued running as fast as the pain in his ribs would allow. The deeper he breathed, the more acute it became. He took a fleeting glance over his shoulder and there was no sign of the man pursuing him, but he kept running until he came to the exit onto the main road. He turned again and looked back along the full length of the path but the man wasn't there.

Stopping to catch his breath, he looked along the road in the direction of the station. But before he set off, he saw a black 4x4 coming towards him. If it hadn't been flashing its lights at the car in front and weaving from side to side attempting to overtake, he would have walked straight towards it. The change of clothes would have made him harder to spot, but the state of his face was still a dead giveaway. He managed to turn away just in time and drop behind a garden wall as the SUV turned sharply right in front of him and sped into the lane, spraying gravel behind it.

At the approach to the train station, he saw a minicab parked outside and, with the promise of an extra tenner on the fare, he was soon being driven away in the direction of home.

By the time the Mitsubishi Warrior had lurched to a halt outside the open door of the lock-up, neither the target nor the copper was anywhere to be seen. A heavy cylinder had rolled to a halt, its rim embedded in an inch of gravel in the middle of the pathway. When George Harris jumped from the passenger seat, he rushed straight past it to the crate that lay on its side in the opening to the garage. On his knees, he raked out the wood shavings and when the crate was empty, he scattered them about him with his hands. Getting to his feet, he looked around at the parts that littered the floor, desperately hoping to find something he knew should have been there. Turning to look through the windscreen of the 4x4, he shook his head. Tommy Riggs swallowed hard and hammered the steering wheel with the heel of his hand.

10.

Jam remembered Herb's message earlier telling him to call back, and as the cab emerged from the Dartford Tunnel, he checked his phone for a signal and returned the missed call. Herb answered on the second ring and asked Jam if he'd been to see his friend.

'He's in a coma.'

'Didn't look good when I left him last night. It was late. There wasn't much I could tell you.'

'Da feds were dere.'

'Who... oh. Oh shit. What did you tell them?'

'What we said... accident.'

'Christ, I should never have involved you in this.'

'Well, I am, man. An' I'm gonna make dis right. I owe it to Jabba.'

'Don't be hasty, son. We don't know what we're up against.'

'I fink it's too late for dat. I went back... to look in dose crates.'

'You did what?'

'It's all metal castin's, spindles and cylinder fings.'

'You shouldn't have done that, lad. That's really going to piss them off.'

'Who are *dey*, man? An' wha's all dat gotta do wiv a truckload of knock-off at a rubbish dump?'

'I'll tell you all you need to know. But for now, you and the girl need to be on your guard.'

'Siobhan? Wha's dis got to do wiv her?'

'They have eyes everywhere. Can you talk to her? Tell her to be careful?'

'For real, but I fink you need to know, someone watch me

earlier. At da garages. Some posh bloke in a suit. Look like he don't belong dere. Nuffink like dose bastards yesterday.'

'Where are you now?'

'Goin' home. I need sleep, man.'

'Of course... Only, if I'd known you were down here, we could have met in Gravesend. A new delivery just came in; you could've given me a hand. It'll take me all night to sort this lot out on my own. You still okay to come down tomorrow?'

'I ain't got no car... you know dat.'

'I'll get Mac to bring you.'

'For real? Dat clown. He's proper dry.'

'Do you want to get paid?'

'Blatantly. Ma aun'ie keep sayin' she ain't no charity.'

'Meet him up there at nine-thirty then.'

'Whatever, man,' Jam said and hung up. He called Siobhan's number and it rang several times before going to voicemail. He left a message asking her to call him and then repeated the words in a text to the same number. He hoped she would look at her phone on her next cigarette break, but he still felt uneasy.

'Change of plan, cuz,' he said to the cabbie. 'Take me Upminster, yeah.' He would take the tube from there.

'Nice one,' came back the reply, with a chuckle. 'I'll be gettin' a nose-bleed soon, this far north of the river!'

An hour later, Jam got off the tube at South Woodford and walked to the café. Brian was at the counter and he only seemed to recognise him after a double-take, and even then, it was probably the bruises he noticed first.

'Are you alright, Jam?' he said. 'Ow is your mate?'

'In a coma. Siobhan still 'ere?'

'I'm sorry to hear that,' he said. 'No, you just missed her.' Jam frowned with disappointment.

'Tired,' he mumbled, and imagined she was probably doing what he planned to do and get a couple of hours' sleep, but Brian didn't seem to hear him.

'Pushin' her luck, she is,' he said. 'No, I'm joking. She got a call from that old fella from yesterday. Wanted to see her up the road again and say thanks for what she did.'

Jam's brain spiked. 'How long ago?'

'Ten minutes, maybe fifteen. It's been a slow afternoon so I said as long as...' Before he could finish the sentence, Jam was out of the door and running across the street with his phone to his ear.

'Herb, sumfink's wrong, man.'

'What is it?'

'Siobhan. Someone call sayin' dey was you an' she went to da house. I'm goin' dere now, yeah. She's not ans'rin' her phone.'

'This is what I was worried about.'

'What?'

'That one of you would be taken.'

'*Taken*? By dem ones yesterday?'

'How long's she been gone?'

'Quarter of a hour. Why would someone take her, man?'

'Soft target, lad. Right, I'm on my way.'

'But it's nuffink to do wiv her.'

'Do you know where she lives?'

'Yeah, I'll go dere after da house.'

'Then call me back.'

'If she not dere... what we gonna do? Not da feds, man. Dis is liber'ies, dough.'

'No! They won't even take it seriously at this stage. Just call me back and we'll deal with this. Understood?'

'Safe.'

The first thing Jam recognised as he turned into the road was the white van. At least that meant Braveheart must be there. When he rattled the door with his knuckles, he heard movement inside. Through the frosted glass, he could see the distorted image of a large figure moving slowly between the rooms either side of the hallway. When he banged harder, the big man finally appeared.

'What?' Mac said, looking down at Jam, his contempt undisguised.

'She here?'

'Who?'

'Siobhan...'

'Huh?'

'Da girl, yer know.'

'The nurse?'

'Yeah, da nurse. She here?'

'No.'

'Dey say she come here to see Herb. You see her, man?'

'Herb isn'ay here.'

'I know dat. It's not what I'm arksing. Have you seen her?'

'I'm busy,' he said, and started to close the door.

'Oi man, mo-o-o-ve!' Jam got a foot in the door but was unable to push it back. 'Did you see her?'

'No. Go 'way.'

'I ain't goin' nowhere, man. Wha'gwun in dere?'

'No your business.'

'You were draggin' sumfink across da hall, man.'

'Piss off!'

'If you don't let me in, man, I'm calling da police.' It was a hollow threat that Jam had no intention of following through, but it was enough to make the heavyweight suddenly step back from the door, causing Jam to fall inward as it opened. Inside, the hall was stacked with boxes and Mac was barely able to squeeze through. Jam followed him into the newly-built area. One of the metal doors was open and the room was still completely bare.

'So you haven't seen da girl?'

'Deaf or stupid?'

'Dey say she comin' here.'

'No here.' Mac cast his eyes sarcastically around the bare passageway.

'Okay,' Jam said, looking through to the kitchen and then turning to the front. 'If you see her, tell Herb, man, innit.'

'Fock yee!'

'Look man, I ain't got no time for dis shit. But when I'm back tomorrow...'

Just then, the phone rang in the front room and the big man pushed past him and disappeared back along the narrow hall. Jam went out into the kitchen where the bowl of pink water and blood-soiled wadding remained untouched on the drainer. Although he could only hear the short, deep grunts echoing down the hall, he guessed Herb was the only person likely to call the landline here, and when Mac lumbered back towards him, Jam suspected he'd been given new instructions.

'Herb's coming,' he said.

'For real.'

'Now go!'

As Jam headed back to the front of the house, he noticed the doors to the rooms either side of the hallway were both shut, which was odd as they'd always been wide open before. He knew the one on the right had the bed in and on the left was a grotty bathroom with a toilet he'd reluctantly had to use during his workdays here. When he went to push on the bedroom door, Mac grabbed his arm and held firmly in a vice-like grip.

'Ma room,' the Scotsman grunted, and glared at him. Maybe even *he* was entitled to some degree of privacy, Jam thought and shrugged. His wrist was released and he turned away. The door to the front room was open and he defiantly put his head around the door only to find it exactly as it had been last night. It was only when he turned and opened the front door that the daylight revealed a faint trail on the floor, partly obscured by the boxes on one side, but that ran along the entire length of the hall. It looked like smeared blood.

'Wha's dat?'

'What?' The big man looked down, suddenly agitated again.

'Is dat blood, man?'

'Go,' he said, and gave Jam a shove out of the door.

Jam stood momentarily in the neglected front garden, and remembered he and Siobhan having to slide Jabba along the floor to get him to Herb's car. It was likely after all his thrashing about that he had started bleeding again. He nodded to reassure himself and got out his phone. His call went straight to voicemail.

***

In the rear seat-well of a stationary car, the backlight of a mobile phone illuminated the words 'Missed Call' and then went off.

***

It was four-thirty when Jam knocked on the door of Siobhan's house. When he heard someone coming, his hopes rose that she would appear, wondering what he was doing there. He hadn't considered what he would say if it wasn't her, so when a man in his late forties looked at him across the threshold, he froze.

'Yes?' the man said.

'Mr Jennin'?'

'Ye-ah,' Siobhan's dad said, eyeing him up suspiciously from head to toe. Jam was getting used to all the shocked expressions he'd been receiving all day when people saw his face, but it took him a while to realise that the look of intrigue in this man's expression had more to do with a familiarity with the clothes he was wearing.

'Is Siobhan dere?'

'No. It's still a bit early for her to be home from work. Who are you?'

'I'm a... friend, Mr Jennin'. We... er, only met recently, but...'

'Are those my clothes?'

'Yeah... I can explain dat... But, I need to know if she phone you dis afternoon.'

'No, I didn't speak to her this morning... and she wouldn't call me... not when I'm sleeping.' Then his expression changed as things started to fall into place, and he added: 'Except for yesterday, when she said she was going out to help a friend. Look, young man, you'd better come inside.'

When Jam followed him into the living room, Minx looked up from her nap and jumped from the warm bed to greet him. It only added to Jennings' bewilderment when the cat purred and rubbed her head against the stranger's leg.

Siobhan woke feeling groggy. She opened her eyes and saw a white ceiling and a fancy light fitting but her vision was blurry and it made her head hurt too much when she tried to focus. Shutting them again, she explored her surroundings with her hands and felt silky sheets. Then she realised her head was on a soft pillow. When she opened her eyes again, there was a woman sitting across the room watching her.

'It's probably best if you stay still.' The woman's voice was deep and distorted but she still sounded gentle and kind as she continued: 'Keep your eyes shut for a little while longer. Whatever they gave you will probably wear off soon.'

As Siobhan's brain started to work through its last conscious memory, it came to the conclusion she must be in a hospital room and the woman was a nurse, keeping an eye on her as she recovered from whatever drug she'd been given by... those men. Yes, the men that jumped out at her as she had walked along the street. Her pulse quickened as she remembered with absolute panic being hooded and bundled into the back of a car, her knees crunching on the metal seat runner as she slipped clumsily into the foot well. Then the sensation of the car as it sped away. Until the needle pierced her arm.

She drifted off again and the next time she opened her eyes, it wasn't the woman sitting across from her.

'Daddy,' she said. 'You're here.' But he didn't get up and he didn't speak. She couldn't understand why he just sat there, rubbing his forehead. She closed her eyes again to stop the room from spinning.

***

Meanwhile, Siobhan's father was standing in the middle of his lounge, looking at the young man dressed in his clothes.

'And your name is?' he asked.

'Dey call me... Jam,' he said, waiting for the look of disdain he usually got from anyone over the age of twenty-nine, but Jennings was confused enough already.

'Well, Jam,' he said, 'Siobhan said she was going out for the evening, but given that you're standing here battered and bruised... in my jeans and jacket... and, it seems, being favoured by my cat, I can only imagine you're some hard-luck story she took pity on and brought home last night. And I take it the blood-spattered hoodie, and the jeans and underwear I found in the bathroom this morning belong to you.'

'I apologise for dat, Mr Jennin'. Siobhan's a good... nurse.' He meant it sincerely but had to push back the image in his head of her riding him like a rodeo gal this morning.

'Indeed,' he said, raising his eyebrows. 'And a heart of gold. Which is fine until people start taking advantage.'

'Look, Mr Jennin'...'

'You'd better start calling me Pete, if those are also *my* shorts you've got on under my jeans.'

'Pete... you know she come to help me and ma bruvver. And cos of dat, she may be involved in sumfink... more dangerous.'

'Oh my God!' The colour drained from Jennings' face. 'What kind of... dangerous?'

'Ma bruvver and me, yeah, got proper bang up by dem.' He pointed to his face. 'Jabba's in hospital.'

'Jabba?'

'Yeah.'

'Who did this to the pair of you?'

'Dunno.'

'Great. So you get in a fight, Siobhan does her Florence Nightingale act, and now you think *she's* in danger?'

'For real. Dat's what I hear. And I go to her café and dey say she gone. She don't answer her phone, you know. So I come here, Mr Jennin'... Pete, to find her.'

'When you say, *that's what you've been told*, told by whom, exactly?'

'He live in Gravesend, yeah, but he's got a place near here.' Jam swallowed hard. 'Dey use it for storage.'

'So, she left work when?'

'About half a hour ago.'

'Okay, Jam. That's not really missing then, is it?' Jennings visibly relaxed as if this no longer ranked highly on his abnormally keen panic scale.

'Dunno,' Jam sighed, trying to embrace Jennings' optimism. Clearly, Pete Jennings was used to measuring unexplained absence in months, and someone not being where you expected them to be after 35 minutes was probably a luxury he would accept every day in return for the torment he must have been going through since the beginning of the year.

'So, we're saying she left work early, and maybe just decided to pop somewhere before coming home, yes?'

'Yeah,' Jam said, and he really wanted to agree and say sorry, he shouldn't have just turned up and worried him like that, especially after everything. But he had no choice. He had to throw one last grenade into Pete Jennings' bunker. 'She say she was goin' to meet someone.'

'Who?' Jennings' eyes came out on stalks.

'Da man from Gravesend... She got a phone call from someone sayin' he was him, but I know it weren't him, yeah, and he's nowhere near here anyway.'

'Okay, Jam. Here's what we're going to do. First, I need to call the office. Then, God knows what Rita will say about keeping Eloise late again after last night, but I'm sure she'll understand...'

***

Losing all sense of time, Siobhan continued drifting in and out. Different people seemed to come and go until the next time she turned to the window, and noticed it was getting darker outside. That was when she realised she could no longer move her arms. And when she tried to raise her knees to help herself sit up, they wouldn't move either. Consciousness finally started to take hold, but it came with the terrifying realisation that her hands and feet were now tied to the four corners of the bed.

After Jennings had arranged for Rita, the childminder, not to bring Eloise back until he phoned her later, he went into the hall and put on his coat.

'You not callin' da feds... da police, man?' Jam said, as he followed him to the door.

'Not yet,' he said. 'I know a few places she sometimes goes after work. I'll go and look first. Do you know this area?'

'Nah. I could come wiv you, dough. Need to make a call first.'

'I was thinking it would probably be better if we split up. You go that way.' Jennings set off up the road and Jam walked in the other direction.

'Herb,' Jam said, when his call was answered. 'She not home.'

'Right,' he said. 'Get back round to Mac and go with him.'

'Go where?'

'He'll know. Just do it. I'll meet you there.'

11.

Siobhan tried to scream but it was just a muffled hum because someone had stretched tape across her mouth. She was sure he wasn't the same man who'd been rubbing his forehead earlier. There was no longer any confusion in her mind about *him* being her father. That man had been a lot shorter when he'd shuffled out of the room with a limp. Whereas this man, now alone with her, he was very tall. And he had a knife.

She wanted to struggle and fight him but the first time she did that, the point of the blade that was slicing effortlessly through the outer seam of her trousers had cut into her leg. Now she was rigid with fear as she felt its unsharpened edge trace a cold line up her thigh towards her waistband.

***

Jam walked up to the van. The rear doors were open and Mac was lifting black plastic sacks into the back.

'Herb say you know where to go, man,' he said, and Mac quickly slammed the doors and turned around.

'Get in!' And as he started the engine, he added, 'I'll fockin' kill 'em.'

'You know dat,' Jam said, fastening the seatbelt.

***

The tall man reached over and slid the blade behind Siobhan's belt and was about to pull on it when the sound of raised voices downstairs made him stop. He cursed as he left the room. She couldn't hear what was being said but it sounded like someone had just arrived. She lay there, one leg exposed and bleeding, her head turned to one side, staring at the knife on the bed.

***

When Pete Jennings walked away from the fourth pub in the area, panic was starting to set in. He'd called Siobhan's mobile half a dozen times in the last two hours and she hadn't picked up or returned any of his messages. He even resorted to texting in case she was somewhere with a poor signal. It was now getting quite late and he needed to phone Rita again but he didn't want to use his mobile in case he missed a call. He headed home in the slightest hope he would find Siobhan sitting in front of the TV, thinking he'd gone to work and oblivious to her phone lying in the bottom of her handbag with a dead battery.

When he got in, the house was empty and there were no messages on the answering machine. Rita needed to drop off Eloise in the next half hour and, after speaking to her, he picked up the phone again, and his finger hovered over the keys. *Was it an emergency when you didn't know where your twenty-two-year-old daughter was at seven o'clock in the evening? Was a crime being committed?* He didn't know. *Was she in danger, a life or death situation?* He was trying hard not to go there. Or were you supposed to call the local police station and hope someone with authority, or at least a sense of urgency, picked it up?

He'd been there before and it was still very raw. He hit 999 and waited for the standard emergency response. He gave the woman as much information as he knew about Siobhan's movements in the last 48 hours, and it hit him hard when he realised how little he did know about what she did, day to day. Or the people she brought home with her. The woman on the phone was particularly interested to know more about the young man he mentioned with the bruises and the story about her being in danger. He could hear her typing as she asked more questions.

'I haven't seen him since we headed in opposite directions

to look for her a couple of hours ago,' he said.

'Can you describe this man, sir?'

'He's average height, maybe taller. Mixed race. Lean but athletic. Curly black hair, brown eyes. His face is badly bruised, as I said.'

'What was he wearing?'

'Levi 501s,' he replied instantly. 'Maroon Ted Baker polo shirt, black M&S pullover, black bomber jacket.'

'You're very observant, sir,' she said. 'Not many people can remember so much detail.'

'And,' he continued, 'he said the fight he'd been in had put his friend in hospital. He had a funny name too. Jabba, I think he said.'

'Okay, sir. I've recorded all of that. Now, what I'd like you to bear in mind is that it is still too soon for you to become overly concerned. In almost every case…' He allowed her to finish her scripted platitudes, even though he wanted to say he'd heard them all before. Only the words *almost every case* repeated in his head. '… the person calls or turns up safe and well. But rest assured, we do still take these reports very seriously and I will despatch a local officer to come and see you later this evening. They may want to take some more details and they will talk you through the process that would then go into effect. Have you got any questions?'

'No,' he said. 'But I should probably tell you before it comes up on some system, this isn't the first time.'

'Sir?'

'That I've had to report…'

'Your daughter has…'

'No. My wife…' There was a moment of silence while the woman thought about her next question, but he resolved her dilemma by adding, '… since January.'

'I'm so very sorry, sir.' The official tone had dropped from her voice. 'You'll know this already, but the best advice I can give is to stay near your phone in case Siobhan calls you. I really hope she does.'

When Rita arrived with the baby, she hugged Jennings and they both cried. She left him with a promise to call later and her certainty that Siobhan would turn up very soon. The cliché about lightning hung in the air, but remained unspoken. Jennings thanked her and took Eloise through to the living room where she fell asleep in his arms. He sat on the sofa and promised her he wouldn't put her to bed until the phone rang.

***

There was an animated conversation underway when the lanky, young man slid conspicuously into the large, modern sitting room.

'Where have you been, Carl?' Ray Riggs asked him.

'Just checking on the girl,' he said hesitantly, before nodding to Terry Pinner and George Harris, who were sitting on either side of the white marble fireplace. Riggs' son, Tommy, was sitting opposite them.

'What happened to you earlier, Tel?' Harris had asked Pinner.

'I went after him, but he was too quick.'

'And then you didn't answer your phone all afternoon,' Tommy chipped in.

'I *have* got a proper job, remember?' Pinner countered, staring back at him. 'I only managed to get back up here tonight because I've got people working for me.'

'I heard you needed a lift because you'd left your car in Romford,' Tommy smirked, and looked at his dad, also grinning.

'That was because I was up there helping you lot out,' Pinner said, directing a look at Riggs before turning back to Tommy. 'And at least my people know how to take orders.'

'What's that supposed to mean?' Tommy threw back at him, but Pinner ignored him and turned back to Harris.

'I found those lads for you, didn't I?'

'Granted, Tel,' Riggs chipped in. 'Nice job you did there.'

'All well and good,' Harris said. 'But it was still lucky we got

112

to the lock-up when we did... what with last week's shipment all over the floor.'

'Yeah, I wanted to ask you about that George, but before I do,' Pinner said, looking up at the tall man who was still standing by the door, 'what girl were you checking on, Carl?'

'The name you gave us,' Riggs cut in.

'Upstairs,' Carl said, leering up to the ceiling.

'What? You just kidnapped her?'

'Two of my men have disappeared, remember?' Riggs said.

'But what's she got to do with that?'

'You tell us, Tel,' Harris said. 'Like Ray said, *you* gave us the names.'

'Yeah, but surely she's not...'

'Forget about her,' Riggs said, cutting across him. 'You were telling me that Herb Long is behind all this.'

'Well, it certainly looks like it could have been his place,' Pinner said. 'Assuming he was using that same name when he bought it.'

'And his gear?'

'More than likely. So, surely he's the one you want, or...'

'We just figured...' Now Tommy butted in, 'maybe we can use her to draw the others in.'

'... or this other guy,' Pinner continued. 'Not some young woman we know nothing about.'

'Oh, right,' Harris chimed in. 'The guy you let get away, Tel. Yeah, that's the one we really want.'

'What was I supposed to do, arrest him? How would that have helped?' Pinner let his point sink in for a moment then decided to shift the subject away from the poor woman he didn't even know, who because of his own actions was now imprisoned by these thugs. 'So, tell me about that shipment, George.'

'It's just the usual, Tel,' Riggs answered. 'Nothing for you to be concerned about.'

'Are you sure about that, Ray? Is that what he told you?' Pinner kept his eyes on Harris, who in turn flashed a nervous look at Tommy.

'What do you mean?' Riggs followed his gaze. 'What does he mean?'

'Like you said, Ray. Just the usual,' Harris said, eyeing Pinner suspiciously.

'There was a document...' Pinner paused and watched Harris' eyes widen. The leather cushion of Tommy's chair creaked as he shifted his weight. 'In the crate that fell open.'

'You've got it, Tel,' Harris said, feigning relief. 'I've been worried sick that little shit got...'

'What document?' Riggs cut across him.

'Tell him what they are, George?'

'Industrial parts,' he said, but his smile looked forced. 'They're all kosher. Top end Venezuelan engineering.'

'That may well be true,' said Pinner. 'Now why don't you tell him where they're going?' Riggs' eyes narrowed as he stared across at Harris, but no one seemed to notice the reflex of Tommy's hand springing up to cover his mouth.

Siobhan remained motionless in her satin prison. She could hear the voices downstairs but couldn't make out anything being said. The longer she lay there, the more she dreaded the moment when that man would return and pick up his knife. She twisted her hands to try to loosen the cords around her wrists but they were too tight. She did the same with her feet but there was no slack there either. She started to panic and began wrenching hard on the bedframe with her arms when the woman stepped back into the room.

'Don't struggle. It'll only be worse for you,' she said, and Siobhan tried to speak. The woman leant over and, before peeling back the tape, said, 'Don't shout, okay?'

'Please help me,' she pleaded.

The woman looked genuinely sorrowful. But when she stuck the tape back and left the room, it was Siobhan's eyes that welled up. The talking continued downstairs and the voices grew louder as she turned her head to the window and gave in to the tears that streamed across her face.

In the sitting room, the discussion was getting heated.

'Are you going to sit there and let this... copper interrogate me in your own sitting room, Ray?' Ray Riggs looked from George Harris to Terry Pinner and then back.

'Answer his question, George.'

Harris dithered for a second, long enough for Tommy to chip in. 'It's all part of that consignment to the Middle East,' he said to his father. 'Those Saudi oil components.' Riggs nodded and looked back at Pinner.

'Now we're getting closer,' Pinner pushed back. 'A bit more halal than kosher, wouldn't you say?'

'So, what's your point, Tel?' Riggs said. 'It's a new contract. We'll be doing a lot of business like that.'

'Maybe so,' Pinner said. 'But the document I saw didn't say anything about Saudi.' Harris shifted uncomfortably in his chair as Tommy shot him a withering glare. Riggs added to his discomfort by staring into his eyes.

'Go on, Tel,' Riggs said.

'How about the Republic of Iraq?'

'So what if it does?' said Harris.

'I wouldn't expect you to know anything about the Non-Proliferation Treaty, George,' Pinner said. 'But surely you've heard about the United Nations, yeah? And the sanctions against Saddam Hussein's weapons of mass destruction?'

'What have you done?' Riggs glared at Harris, and the look of horror on Tommy's face changed to mimic the accusatory stare of the patriarch.

'Ray, don't sweat it,' Harris said, but he was the one starting to perspire. 'It's not like we'll just put it on a ship and set sail for Baghdad.'

'Oh, okay,' Pinner added, piling on the pressure. 'You'll find some way of getting it in as humanitarian aid, will you? And don't tell me you paid for the import from South America in dollars?'

'What if we did?' Harris said, and Tommy's eyes widened.

Pinner watched as Riggs turned to Harris, shaking his head.

'I might be able to navigate a few domestic obstacles for you, Ray...' Pinner said.

But Riggs didn't wait for him to finish. 'You fucking moron, George.'

Tommy managed a sly grin and Pinner smirked. He couldn't have put it better himself.

The touch of a hand on her arm was like an electric shock, but when she turned, it was the woman again. She had picked up the knife from the bed and was reaching across to cut the cord from Siobhan's wrist. In no time, both her hands were free and she sat up as her feet were being released. Her head spun from the sudden movement and she wasn't sure if she'd be able to stand without collapsing, but the woman sensed her anxiety and put an arm around her.

'Thank you,' she whispered and the woman nodded. Silently, she led her onto a large mezzanine overlooking a grand stairwell, and now the voices below were much louder. At the top of the stairs, they heard footsteps across the tiled floor and saw one of the men walk towards the huge entrance door. The woman pulled her back out of sight and into another room.

It was a large dressing room with built-in units on either side. At the end of the central space was another door and the woman led her into a private bathroom. She opened the French door on the far wall and Siobhan looked out over the dark shadows cast by a landscaped garden. The drop to the ground was too far to jump without risking serious injury, but there was a narrow balcony and the woman helped her out onto it.

'Stay here,' she said, looking deep into Siobhan's eyes. 'I'll distract them and try to get them to leave so you can come back down the stairs. But if you have to jump from the balcony, do it. At least you'll have a chance that way.'

'Thank you,' Siobhan said.

'Don't thank me yet. If they catch you, he'll make me... prove I didn't help you,' the woman said, looking down at the knife she was still holding. 'Take this, you might need it.'

***

The traffic was crawling and the brake lights of the car in front lit up the rain-spotted windscreen as the wipers dragged an intermittent smear across the glass. The big man pummelled the wheel impatiently as the van jolted back and forth, causing its strange cargo to slide around noisily.

Jam's phone rang and he could see it was Herb. 'Where are you, man?' he said, wasting no time with a greeting.

'Ten minutes away,' he said. 'Maybe longer in this traffic.'

'Wh'appen when we get dere?'

'First challenge will be getting anywhere near the house. We'll need to play it by ear. There's usually someone keeping watch. But if they've got her there, it could be like Fort Knox.'

'I'm tellin' you man, if dey da people what bang us up in Cha'ham, and dey got her, yeah, you ain't never holdin' me back.'

'There's a time and place for heroics. It's also a sure way of getting killed. So let's just see what we're up against first.'

'See you dere.'

***

When the landline rang, Eloise opened her eyes momentarily, wrinkled her face and buried it back into her daddy's arm.

'Siobhan?'

Pete Jennings' hopes were dashed when it was a man's voice who responded. 'I'm DC Melville, sir. Metropolitan Police. Calling back about your daughter.'

'Have you found her?'

'No. I'm sorry, sir. It's still very early days, but don't be alarmed. I wanted to follow up with you about the man you said you spoke to this evening.'

'Jam?'

'Yes, that's him, sir. And you said he had a friend in hospital after a fight. Is that right?'

'That's what he said. Jubba, I think he called him.'

117

'That's not his real name, but he *is* in a coma at Oldchurch. I spoke to a man calling himself Jam this morning. His real name is Kingston Michaels and he had come there to see his friend. He gave a statement to the effect that the other man's injuries resulted from an occupational accident. Is there anything else you can tell me that might help us understand what's really going on here?'

'The first I knew of it was when Siobhan called me yesterday, saying she was going out for the evening. I now know she was going to help these two young men who'd been badly hurt. She's always offering to help hopeless causes. Just a second,' he said, and cradled the phone with his chin while gently putting Eloise in her recliner. 'She was training to be a nurse until her mother... she had to quit. Anyway, when I got in from work this morning, she'd had someone back here last night – there was blood on some clothes in the bathroom – and then this guy turns up at my door in my own jeans. He told me there had been a fight and that another man in Kent somewhere... Gravesend, I think it was, had warned him today that as a result, he and Siobhan were both in danger and he wanted to warn her. Now she's disappeared, I don't know what to think.'

'Okay, sir. You've been very helpful. Let me give you my number and if you think of anything else or you hear from Siobhan, or any of these men, please give me a call back.'

'Is someone still coming out to see me later?'

'Er... yes, sir. If that's what you were told. It probably won't be me, though.'

***

The front door was still open but Terry Pinner had walked too far out onto the driveway to hear Natalie Riggs as she came down the stairs.

'She's gone!' she shouted. 'The girl's escaped.'

Carl was the first to come running out of the sitting room and he met her in the hall.

'Gone? How?' he yelled.

Ray Riggs was a few paces behind him and looked at his wife questioningly. 'How could she get away?' he asked.

'Looks like she got the knife.'

'What knife?' he hissed.

'His,' she said, pointing at Carl, who was now bounding up the stairs, two at a time. 'I saw him leave it on the bed.'

'You idiot!' Riggs shouted after him, and started to hobble up the stairs himself.

'Don't go upstairs!' she screamed. 'She must have come down here while you've all been in there arguing. She's probably out in the road by now.' At that, Riggs decided not to struggle with the stairs any further and both men came back down and followed George Harris out through the front door.

When Riggs reached the road, he looked both ways and saw Terry Pinner getting in his car.

'Did you see her leave?' he said, his voice lowered to a deep, angry whisper.

'See who?' Pinner turned and glared at him.

'The girl, you fool. The one we've just been talking about.'

'No I didn't,' Pinner said, looking around him. 'But out here... in the real world, let's get one thing straight about where I stand, Ray. If I did see a young woman running down the street, distressed and in danger, I'd be obliged to help her. I hope you can understand that.'

'Just don't push your luck, copper,' Riggs said, and shuffled back towards the house.

12.

Siobhan clung to the balcony railing at the side of the doorframe and tried to stay out of sight from within the bathroom. Even with her trousers sliced open all up one leg, she didn't notice the evening was turning colder.

She was still in a state of shock, but relieved to finally be alone and outside in the air. She tried to peer back into the room but there was little to see beyond the voile curtain that the woman had pulled back before she left to raise her diversionary alarm.

The back of the house was quiet as she looked down on the garden but she could hear nothing of what was happening inside or around the front. She imagined that the woman would be trying to cause a commotion out there to give her more chance to get away unnoticed. But without the option of jumping safely onto the paved area below, she was going to have to risk going back in at some point.

She waited for what seemed like hours, but after maybe ten minutes, she turned the handle slowly. As the door opened inwards, the breeze drew the voile out into the air and she held it back and stepped inside. Before she took a second step, she heard voices downstairs and froze. If they hadn't left the house yet, how was she supposed to get out? Footsteps coming up the stone staircase sent her back into a panic and she went back outside and closed the door.

A few minutes later, along the street, the van's lights and ignition were snuffed and the vehicle eased to a stop. Jam got ready to jump out, but without knowing which house they were heading for, he turned to Mac.

'Come on, man, let's go an' get her.'

'Wait.'

'For what?'

'Herb.'

'Nah, man. If she in dere, I'm goin' in.'

'Have tee wait.'

'You know dat. But I'm goin' in. Which one?'

A chunky finger was pointed further along the street. 'White one,' he said.

As Jam got out and headed towards the house, the words 'Fockin' bawbag!' hung in the damp evening air.

As he walked along the pavement, Jam started to realise just how big all the houses were in this street. All set back from the road with wide, sweeping driveways behind high walls and heavy, electronic gates. The white one was alone in having lights on upstairs, and when he got within twenty yards, he started to realise he may have been hasty going it alone.

Although he could see the main gate was closed, the pedestrian access at the side was open, and he slowed his pace as he approached. There didn't seem to be anyone in the front garden and he slipped through the gate and headed for the shadows of the large shrubs and conifers that lined the boundary with the next property.

Beneath the grand overhang of a pillared porch, he noticed the imposing entrance door was open and he edged closer to the front wall so he could approach from the side and duck below the large bay window on the left. At that moment, a man came through the door and stood under the porch, staring out into the darkness. Jam instantly recognised him as the little bastard who had put Jabba into a coma.

As the man lit a cigarette, Jam clenched his fists and wondered how he could lure him out into the open. He knew he would lose his advantage if he had to take him on inside the house, as there were others who would come to his aid. He reached down and picked up a stone, and threw it back at the side gate, where it clanged noisily against the metal post.

It was enough to alert the smoker, who instantly dropped his cigarette and came out into the drizzling darkness. Jam stayed in the shadows as the man walked past him and reached the gate. The short man looked left and right along the road as Jam silently followed and stopped two paces behind him. When the man turned to walk back in, Jam let fly with the biggest right cross he'd ever delivered.

Unlike in the ring, where an opponent would usually be ready for any punch, this man had unknowingly turned right into it, doubling the energy carried in its downward trajectory. It connected with the force of a club-hammer against his left temple. His head shot back like a piston and, apart from the dull thud of impact, the only other sound was the crack from his neck as his right cheekbone made a hideously unnatural contact with his shoulder. Under the momentum of the blow, he hit the pavement sideways and didn't move again.

Jam knew it was a devastating blow and there was little point taking any further risk standing out in the open. Much as he wanted to avenge Jabba further by heeling the man's face into the gravel, he resisted and slipped back into the shadows. As he reached the porch and looked through the open door, he was sure there was no other sound or movement inside, but he knew as soon as he went in, he would be exposed to the harsh glare of the illuminated entrance hall and the white marble staircase.

He found the courage to slip through the entrance and into the first room he found on the right. It was a cavernous sitting room, which, like the hall, was almost entirely white, apart from some oversized modern artwork around the perimeter and an equally massive TV that gave the impression of a giant black hole on the inside wall.

He felt almost as exposed in there as he had been in the hall, and when he saw another door at the far end of the room, he headed towards it. The door was ajar and now he could hear voices. He moved to the side so he could see through the gap. He saw a middle-aged man limping back and forth. As he moved to the side, Jam saw a woman sitting on a chair.

'When we find her,' the man said in a deep, hushed but threatening voice, 'you're going to show me you didn't help her escape.' With that, he backhanded her across the face.

Jam's instinct was to go in and teach the bully a lesson, but he was almost grateful for what the man had said. In those few seconds, he'd learned that Siobhan had been there, and now she had got away. He no longer needed to stay in this house; he could go and look for her outside. But by the time he returned to the door nearest the hall, there were more voices coming down the stairs.

***

DI Pinner hadn't made much progress through the heavy traffic when his phone rang.

'Terry?'

'Yes, love.'

'Are you heading home soon?' his wife asked. 'I heard you come in last night... but you were off before I woke this morning.'

'On my way, but the traffic's awful. Can't see me getting there any time soon.'

'Oh, okay, never mind then.'

'About what?'

'I thought you said you would come with me to Simon's school open evening. But if you're not going to be here in time...'

'I'm sorry, Gillian. It completely slipped my mind. Tell him I'll make it up to him. Maybe his big sister will go with you?'

'I doubt it... and you know she doesn't like you calling her that. Teenage girls... bad enough... without what she's been through.'

'Tell you what, I'll ring when I'm closer and if I can't make it, I'll meet you after and treat the pair of them to pizza.'

'Okay, that's something I suppose. See you later.'

When he ended the call, the thought of the kids wouldn't leave his mind. His son was such a geeky, little boy; he sometimes wondered whether he was really his. And the girl...

she had been a real handful early on. Not that they hadn't been warned. But she'd settled down in recent years. The cost in terms of his secret debt to Riggs might have been great, but she was starting to become a daughter he could be proud of. She also seemed to have a calming influence on his wife's increasing mood swings, which made their relationship marginally more bearable. Good-looking kid too; at seventeen she was turning into a real catch for some lucky lad. He just wasn't sure he was prepared yet to be the protective father figure when she started bringing home zit-faced, little gob-shites who only wanted to get into her Calvin Kleins.

Thinking of young girls falling prey to gob-shites, he had no idea who the girl was that he'd unwittingly led Riggs' men to kidnap. And here he was driving away when she was no doubt scared and hiding, in fear for her life. He wasn't a particularly compassionate man, and he had a great deal to lose if he was seen to help her, but the more he thought about it, perhaps there was something he could do where the risk was manageable. Mulling it over as he continued to crawl along in the endless queue of cars, he contemplated how fortune seemed to be turning in his favour.

Indeed, some would have called it a stroke of luck, but to him, good instincts had led him to Oldchurch Hospital that morning. To have then observed that half-cast, covered in bruises, and discovered the names of all the persons of interest, was a triumph of old-fashioned detective work. The trouble was, when he did that for the job, a slap on the back was the best he could expect. At least when he did it for himself, the material gain was usually just enough to obscure the nagging dilemma he'd otherwise find hard to ignore. And the events that had unfolded later that day had now presented him with an opportunity to expose Harris' treachery whilst showing Riggs, that old cripple, he could still deliver.

With that boost of self-confidence, he found the number and made the call.

'Melville,' was the terse reply.

'Evening, Constable. This is DI Pinner, how are you, Jim?'

'Oh, good evening, sir. Yes, I'm well, thanks. On a bit of a run-around to be honest, but all in all, can't grumble. What can I do for you, sir?'

'Your application, Jim. It's sitting with the AC and I've given him my recommendation.'

'Well, thank you, sir. I'm really hoping I can get this move.'

'Not the reason for the call, though, Jim. I was wondering if you could check something out for me this evening. I've just come through your manor and need to get back home. But I think there was something strange going on. I'd call it in but it's in my Chief Constable's neighbourhood and I don't want to cause a big fuss that might embarrass him. It might even have been his house. But as it's your patch, I wondered if you could take a look. On the QT, like... just between us.'

'Er... that's a bit... awkward, isn't it, sir. Really, I'd need to go through the proper...'

'Melville... I need to know I can trust you with things like this. If... and it is still *if*... this transfer goes through, you'll need to get used to the fact outside the Met, you sometimes have to do things a bit more... spontaneously. We don't have the manpower you guys have. I need to know you can be... creative when the need arises. Do this for me and that will give me real confidence in you.'

'So, what was it exactly that you saw?'

'I think there may be a young lady in a spot of difficulty. I thought I saw her running from the house. Like I said, heaven forbid it was the one belonging to the big cheese. But I might have it all wrong and that's why I don't want to be heavy-handed. Just go and take a look, will you? I'd do it myself but I need to get home for the kids. No blues and twos. Just a bit of old-fashioned neighbourhood policing. Can you do that for me?'

'Well, sir, this is really strange...'

'Either you want this transfer, or you don't, Constable...'

'No, sir... It's not that. It's just that I'm currently looking into a missing person report involving a young lady who

126

disappeared in the area only this afternoon. I know that sounds like a bit of a coincidence, but I'll definitely check it out, sir. If you can give me the address, I'll head right over there.'

'Good man, Jim. Have you got a pen?'

***

The nape of her neck was starting to feel the chill in the air as she backed up tight against the wall beside the doorframe. Her priority was to stay concealed, but she was now aware of the fine drizzle that was beginning to make the ledge slippery underfoot. Even with the door shut, Siobhan could now hear shouting inside, and after ten or twenty seconds, she continued to resist the burning temptation to turn around. When it was quiet again, she looked obliquely across the window glass and her heart almost stopped when she saw the dark outline of someone on the other side.

She looked down at the drop and prepared for the moment she would have to clamber over the wet railing and risk the jump. And that's when she noticed the corner of the sheer material by her feet. The voile was trapped under the door. If the person on the other side tried to pull the curtain back, it would catch and they would know the door had been opened.

Jam's greatest fear about being in this large room with a door at either end was starting to come to fruition. He could continue to hide behind the door to the hallway, but if either of the two men who had come down the stairs walked straight in, he could only remain hidden behind the door for so long. If they touched the door at all, he would be in big trouble. Equally, if anyone from the side room at the back came in, they would see him straight away.

He stood there anyway; he had no other choice. When the footsteps of the men in the hall grew louder, he braced himself, but then they stopped and he could hear them talking. Turning his head very slightly, he was able to see one of them through the hinged slit in the door. It was the man who had beaten him the previous day but he couldn't see who he was talking to.

'I've had another look upstairs,' he said. 'Nothing.'

'I stood dere, jus' inside dat door, whole time we was in dere with Pinna, right up till he left.' The other voice was younger, with an accent Jam knew didn't belong in this part of town. 'I'm tellin' ya, no way she wen' out da front door. Gotta be out da back.'

'The side gate's locked and the only other way out to the road is back through the house. If she's out there, she's got no other way through. We'll put the floodlights on and flush her out.'

'D'ya see Tommy upstairs?'

'He went out for a... Hang on, what's that on the step? Looks like he dropped it.'

'He's hardly smoked it. Where is he? What's that by the gate?'

'Tommy?' one of them yelled.

Jam heard them both run out the front door and he took the only opportunity he was likely to get to leave the room. As he crossed the hall, a door along the downstairs corridor started to open and the man who had hit the woman in the back room limped out. By then, Jam had made it to the stairs and had to go up them and around the upstairs landing to stay out of the man's line of sight. When he got to the top, he watched as the man shuffled out the front door after the other two.

He stood there for a split second, weighing his options. If they hadn't been able to find Siobhan after searching a house they knew, what chance did he have? The woman was his only chance. As quietly as he could on the balls of his feet, he ran back down the stairs and into the room at the back. He shut the door behind him and went to the woman who was holding her face. She looked up with a start and he held up his hands.

'Don't scream,' he said.

'Who the hell are you?' she hissed back.

'I can help.'

'Pah!' she grunted. 'You can, can you?'

'I see what he did to you.'

'And if you care,' she said, 'for both our sakes, you'll get out before he comes back.'

'You know where she is, dough? Da girl? Her name's Siobhan. Did you help her?'

'And how will telling you that help me?'

'Look, dey did dis to me.' He pointed to his face. 'Don't let dem do da same to her.'

'You think they would stop at a few bruises?'

'I can stop dem. For real, I'll come back an' help you.'

'It's too late for me. I made my bed...'

''S'never too late. I can get you outta dis.'

'You don't know what you're saying.'

'Is it? I gotta go before he come back. But let me help *her*... please?' She stared back at him and he shook his head and turned away.

'Upstairs, second door,' she whispered. 'Behind the dressing room, on the bathroom balcony.'

'Fank you,' he said, and left her alone.

13.

The Mercedes pulled into a gap at the kerb on the opposite side of the road to where Mac was still sitting in the van. Herb got out and came around to his window.

'Where's the lad?'

'Gone in.'

'What did I tell you?'

'Not ma problem.'

'It will be when we have to go in and scrape him off the floor. How long ago?'

'Ten minutes... fifteen?'

'Have you seen anything since?'

'Nothing.'

'Right, come on. Let's go and take a look.'

They walked side by side towards the house but stopped short when they saw two men crouched over the prone body of a third. Blood ran in tributaries down the slope of the pavement and collected in a dark pool in the gutter.

'At least we now know how he got in,' Herb whispered, and Mac huffed with what could have been disdain or respect.

They watched as the two men started lifting their fallen colleague, and when another man came to help them, Herb's eyes narrowed.

'Riggs,' he whispered, and Mac huffed again.

After the three of them had carried the other one back towards the house, Herb and Mac made their way into the front garden and took up positions in the bushes on either side of the concourse.

***

Melville was still far from convinced this was the right thing for him to be doing as he pulled up behind a white van in the street Pinner had told him to go to. Going alone to an incident reported by a senior officer who didn't want to make it official but who held his career in the palm of his hands had a very sleazy feel to it. And if it wasn't for the coincidence with the disappearance of Siobhan Jennings, he would have driven past slowly and at the end of the road, texted the Detective Inspector to say he'd found nothing suspicious to investigate further before heading home.

But he now felt he also owed it to Pete Jennings to keep an open mind and complete a comprehensive assessment of the situation as he found it. As for reporting back to Pinner, he would then be in a better position to complete a written report for his potential new boss and demonstrate that he was capable of exercising operational judgement that might fall outside the sometimes overly-strict parameters that modern-day risk management protocols demanded.

The address Pinner had given was the Chief Constable's. Melville tried to maintain a disinterested air as he approached the entrance to the imposing redbrick pile. There were no lights on at the front and when he found the drive was devoid of any cars, it started to look like there was no one home. However, the houses along this street were so huge, it was certainly possible for a large house party to be happening at the rear without being apparent at the front. He took a few steps through the gate towards the front door when a security light flooded the entire driveway, leaving him exposed in its harsh, judgemental glare.

He paused momentarily, but by then it was too late; he realised he couldn't just turn back. He continued walking towards the entrance, and when he got to the steps leading up to the door, his suspicion was confirmed when he saw the small camera suspended below the pillared overhang. He nodded towards it and held up his warrant card to identify himself, and pressed the door chime button. After a minute or so, he turned and walked away. As he suspected, no one was home and he would now have to be ready to explain his actions to the boss of the boss of the man who held his career in the palm of his hands.

Back on the pavement, he turned to walk back to the car when he noticed a shadow thrown by the security light in the shape of a giant, and when he looked back at the bushes on that side of the front garden, he saw a large man with a crew cut staring back at him. In the second it took him to make out the features, the light went off and the hedge was plunged back into darkness.

'Who's there?' he demanded, but there was no reply. 'Come out of there now. I'm a police officer. And you're trespassing.'

As he looked through the heavy, metal gate into the frontage of the property next to the one he'd just walked away from, he could see the front door was open and he headed towards the pedestrian gate on the other side. Maybe it was just a nosy neighbour, after all, looking out for the Chief Constable next door. But as he approached the narrow opening, the streetlight picked out rivulets on the pavement that shone like tar. He took the white handkerchief from his pocket and knelt down to dab the liquid. It was obvious what it was. He reached for his phone.

***

Jam got halfway up the stairs before he heard the men shuffling in from the porch. Had one of them looked, they would have seen him take the last few steps, but they were too concerned for the injured man and carried him straight into the sitting room. At the top of the stairs, Jam crossed the landing to the second door and entered the dark, narrow room at the back of the house. He closed the door behind him and felt his way along the row of fitted closets until he came to the end and saw another door, which he pulled open and entered the bathroom.

In the sitting room, blood was soaking into the cream carpet and Ray Riggs called his wife from the back room.

'Make yourself useful, woman!' he shouted, as Natalie came

through the side door. 'Come and take a look at Tommy.'

George Harris stood and watched as Riggs cradled Tommy's head. 'Who the hell did this?'

'Whoever it was can only be here for one reason.'

'Do you think he's already inside?'

Riggs shrugged and looked across at his wife as she knelt the other side of their son. 'Did you see anyone come in?' he said. She shook her head without looking up. 'Well go and get some towels. And while you're out the back, unlock the strong room and switch on all the outside lights. And for God's sake, bring some cold water back with you before that blood leaves a stain.'

She got up and scurried away, and Riggs turned back to Harris. 'Go with her, George. Bring some hardware and check again upstairs while I go and look out the back with Carl.'

Harris followed Natalie to the strong room and handed out pistols and ammunition on his way back through to the hall. Siobhan gripped the railing with one hand and the knife in the other, hoping for her fight or flight instincts to decide what she would do next. Just then, beneath her, the garden and the entire back wall of the house was illuminated like a stage, and she was left standing on the balcony like a Shakespearian leading lady in the spotlight.

Jam turned and stood at the French doors and tried peering out through the net curtain just as the outside area lit up with an array of blinding floodlights. He jumped to one side and tried to pull back the curtain enough to look out, but it snagged at the bottom corner of the door. He then thought he saw movement and slowly lowered the handle and pulled the door inward. As he did, Siobhan swung around from behind the wall and he grabbed her hand before the knife she was gripping could come down into his chest. When she saw it was him, she dropped the knife and launched her arms around his neck.

'Quick, inside.' As he pulled her in, she slumped to the floor. He sat with her on the tiles, holding her tight as she began to sob. ''S'okay, baby. I got you.' he whispered. 'Dey gonna pay for dis, for real. Dis never shoulda happen.'

'I'm okay,' she said, and tried to smile.

'You bleedin',' he said, and she looked down at her leg and shook her head as if that was nothing. 'I get you outta here.'

'Take this,' she said, handing him the knife. 'It's you he really wants. He just wanted to play with me.'

'Bastard! Which one.'

'He's really tall. Is he the one who did this to you?' she said, gently touching his face.

'Nah. But he did dat to you. When I finish wiv him, he wish he never bin born.'

Melville's first instinct was to call for backup, but of all the times to have reasonable cause to initiate a full-blown police presence, and of all the places, this was starting to feel like the kind of dilemma they just didn't train you for at Hendon.

'DI Pinner,' was the response when his call was answered.

'Sir, it's DC Melville. I'm at the scene... where you said, sir.'

'Good man, Jim. Anything to report?'

'Nothing from the Chief Constable's property, sir, but...'

'What is it?'

'Next door, sir. Blood on the pavement. Quite a lot. I thought I'd let you know before I raise the alarm.'

'Oh shit!' Pinner sighed. 'Okay, Jim. Good work. You've done the right thing calling me first. What else can you see?'

'There was someone in the bushes, sir.'

'The young woman?'

'No. A man... really big guy. I thought he was just watching me from next door, but he's no longer there... Shall I go in, sir?'

'No, Jim. I want you to keep watching for me and keep a safe distance. I'm going to turn around and head back.'

'I thought you had a family commitment, sir.'

'Yeah... I did. Joy of the job, though, isn't it, Jim? Always on duty. Just don't go in until I get there.'

'You're sure you don't want me to get some more backup, sir, for when you get here?'

'No, let's not be hasty. I'm sure there's more to this than

meets the eye, Constable. And I want to know what we're dealing with before anything gets out of hand.'

'If you say so, sir.'

The tall shrubs kept Mac well hidden. He was grateful when next door's front light went out and put him back into darkness. He preferred to remain in the shadows, but more than that, he didn't like to fall under the scrutiny of the filth. He watched as the copper made his call and suspected that within minutes, he'd hear sirens and the place would be awash with blue lights. He decided it would be better to make a move now and risk being seen by this one pig, than hang around and have to deal with a whole drove of the bastards.

He could either wait for him to pass on his way to the front door and brazenly walk across the drive to the gate, or he could try and squeeze through the branches and make his way back towards and along the front wall. Either way, he'd have to get across to the smaller gate because he'd have no chance getting his frame over the main one. But, to his surprise, having finished the call, instead of coming through the gateway, the copper retreated and walked back in the direction from which he'd originally come. Mac now took his chance and, skirting around the edge of the driveway, made it to the gate.

The only person to see him slip through the exit and head back towards his van was Herb, who knew from past experience that Mac had a particular dislike for the boys in blue. Herb remained in position close to the front of the house and continued to watch for signs of activity. As far as he was aware, Jam and Siobhan were still inside, but he was now going to have to rely on Jam to get her out.

When Mac saw the copper get into a car right behind his van, he thought he would just drive away. Mac would then have to decide whether to make his escape anyway, or go back and support Herb. But, when the pig just sat there looking down the street, he had no choice but to stay where he was and watch from behind another garden fence.

Once up the stairs, Harris pointed his gun at the second door. The closer he got, the clearer he could hear voices, and he slowed his movement and reached for the handle.

He stepped through into darkness and edged his way towards the bathroom door, behind which the sound of talking was now more distinct. When he grabbed the door quickly and pulled it inwards, the room was bathed in light from outside, and he swept the gun from one side to the other.

The only thing out of place was the curtain pulled back at the French doors and instead of voices, he now heard the jingle of a radio news bulletin coming from the speaker set in the ceiling.

Stupid woman, he thought, as he opened the door onto the balcony and looked down into the garden, where he saw Riggs limping around the shrubbery. He lowered the pistol and walked back through the bathroom to check on the next room.

Jam was relying on two things when the man he now recognised as the bastard who'd jumped him and then banged him up yesterday walked past. First, that his guard would be down enough so that his grip on the gun, now pointed at the ground, would have loosened. Second, that the sound of the closet door slamming behind him would make him turn, but not so quickly that he would be able to aim and fire. It had been Siobhan's idea and he hadn't had time to disagree with her.

She watched through a gap in the closet door and saw him pass in front of her. When he was framed in the doorway against the light from the mezzanine, she kicked the closet door from inside as hard as she could with her good leg and it crashed back on itself against the adjacent panel. He turned quickly and for an awful moment, she looked down the barrel of his gun until another closet door shot out like a battering ram and sent the man backwards, hard against the wall as the gun clattered across the floor.

In no time, Jam was on him and with each punch, the man's face became soft beneath his fists. It was no contest when the man beneath him failed to get his arms up from under Jam's legs.

Pinned to the floor and with no defence, he was unconscious by the fifth blow. Jam hit him several more times until Siobhan put a hand on his shoulder.

She took his hand as they headed down the stairs, and when they reached the bottom, he turned to look towards the back room. Standing in the doorway with a bloody towel in her hand was the woman who had helped them. Siobhan smiled and Jam held up his hand, but she scowled back at them.

'That's my boy in there,' she hissed, pointing to the sitting room. And with that, she turned her head in the direction of the back garden and let out an ear-piercing scream.

Siobhan pulled on Jam's hand and they both ran through the front door. Outside, Herb saw them coming and stepped out to reassure them. He took Siobhan's hand and she went with him through the gate. She lost her grip on Jam as Herb pulled her along the pavement. She didn't look back until they reached the car.

Everything seemed to slow down. She was aware of Herb pushing her into the front seat and slamming the door. She saw him run around the front to the driver's side and get in beside her. And as she shouted out for Jam, he started the engine and pulled away.

When they passed the gate, in a blur of panic and confusion, there was no sign of Jam running towards them. But as they sped past, she turned and saw the man who had cut her standing in the front drive, looking down. He was laughing.

Jam felt the impact before he heard the thud. His whole body twisted as his left shoulder was propelled forwards. The blade sliced through muscle and cleaved into the bone where its point snapped off and the fragment pierced deeper. For a second, the pain was immense, and then there was an eerie silence as he spun to the ground and landed on his right side. His body felt paralysed but for his right hand, which instinctively gripped his left arm. He looked up as the outline of a figure appeared into his peripheral vision. As Jam's brain began to focus, he saw the sneering smile. But what shocked him more about those eyes leering down at him was that he recognised them.

'Oh my days!' the man said and laughed. The accent was unmistakeably LonJam. Its origin, Croydon. His name, Carlton Parr, was the last on Jam's list of his friend's childhood tormentors. 'Alright, Michaels? Long time, man. Ain't dat a touch. Now you da one gettin' shank, yeah. An' wha'bout de Fornton Heaf massif? Ya big-arse dappy cuz, man? 'Ow's Jabba da Hut?'

14.

As the Mercedes sped past, Melville started his car, reversed into a driveway and pulled away after it in a single smooth manoeuvre. He'd seen the older man leading the girl from the house and then bundle her into his car, and now was the time for his instincts to supersede any unofficial orders he was operating under from Pinner. Had he looked in his rear-view mirror as he accelerated down the street, he would have seen the big guy finally emerge from a neighbouring garden and head to the white van he'd been parked behind.

The Mercedes had to slow at a junction and he almost got up behind it before it turned right into the main road. The congestion from earlier was now receding and traffic was returning to normal. The consequence for Melville was that the two lanes he needed to cross now had a continuous flow of cars and he had to wait precious seconds before he could risk pulling out. It was only a small gap but he pulled forward and the approaching driver rebuked his impatience with the flashing of lights and the blaring of his horn. Melville then had to sit straddling the lane with the driver becoming more and more irate while a gap opened up in the far lane. He ignored the motorist, who in spite of the rain was now leaning out of his window, gesturing with combinations of fingers in Melville's general direction.

Up ahead, he could see the Mercedes indicating right again and now, *it* had to contend with the oncoming traffic. This time, when Melville indicated to follow it, he was able to pull up right behind it. He could see the driver and passenger engaged in highly dramatic conversation and Siobhan seemed to be pleading with the man. With both cars stationary, Melville started getting out of his, but when an oncoming vehicle flashed for the Mercedes to cross, he had to react quickly to get back in and pull away behind it through the same gap. When he did so, the flash he received was not such a friendly gesture.

Now that they were back into quieter streets, he put on the blue lights that were built into the car's customised indicator housing. As he followed the Mercedes through a series of turns, it seemed to slow down but didn't stop. The name of the road they were in didn't register with him until the girl looked back through the rear window and held up her hand with a thumbs-up gesture. He then remembered the address he'd been given for Pete Jennings in the event he was able to pay a visit later that evening. When the Mercedes finally indicated to pull in at the same house number, he switched off the lights and drew up behind it.

The girl got out of the car and walked towards him, and he lowered his window in a strange reversal of protocol.

'I'm okay,' she said. 'He brought me home. You need to go back and help Jam.'

'Who?' he said, but she just turned towards the house where the front door had now opened and ran towards the man walking down the path. When she got to him, they hugged.

Melville had no time to take any satisfaction from the reunion. He knew DI Pinner was on his way to the other house, so he turned his car around and headed back the way he came.

Herb watched the copper drive away with some relief, and noticed how he seemed to be talking, presumably on a car phone. That prompted Herb to reach for his own mobile.

'The girl's safe at home,' he said, when Mac answered. 'The copper followed us here, but he's going back to the house now. I need you to try to get the lad out before he arrives. This time, he's not likely to be alone.'

'Yes, boss,' Mac said, before muttering '*Fockin' hell*' under his breath as he ended the call and headed back to the house where the front garden was now deserted and the entrance door was shut.

Pete Jennings' bomber jacket had been pulled down around Jam's wrists behind him and he was now slumped in the chair in the back room where the woman had been sitting when he'd seen her getting abused earlier. Now she was the one slapping him.

The tip of the knife that had broken off was still embedded in his shoulder and with every movement, it shifted spitefully against the bone. He had almost passed out when the man he'd recognised from his school days had pulled him up by his arm and dragged him into the house.

'You know this piece of shit, Carl?' Ray Riggs said.

'Blatantly, man. We go way back,' Carlton Parr replied with a sinister laugh. 'Shoulda sent *me* down to Cha'ham, Ray. Coulda had some fun wiv his likkle, fat boo.'

'But what have these two got to do with all this anyway?'

'Less arks him, yeah,' Parr said. 'When da missus finish.'

'That's enough from you,' Riggs said to Natalie. 'Make yourself useful and go and check on Tommy. See if you think we need to call the doc.'

After she left the room, Parr waved the broken point of his knife close to Jam's face and walked behind him. But instead of using the knife, he positioned the heel of his free hand over the ragged puncture. Jam pushed back against the chair and his face contorted with the pain as Parr ground his palm into the wound so that the metal tip inside bit deeper into bone.

'Right then, Michaels,' Riggs said, leaning to stare into Jam's eyes. 'You'd better tell us what you've been up to. Let's start with Herb Long, shall we? Who is that piece of shit to you?'

Before he could even decide whether to answer, Parr gouged his shoulder again and Jam's jaw clenched. As the pain eased, he opened his mouth to speak. It was too dry to spit in the older man's face and the best he could do was pretend to whisper in order to draw him closer. Then he shouted as loudly as he could.

'Fuck you!'

The jolt of his head when Riggs punched him made his neck twist and the pain in his jaw was drowned out by the agony of his shoulder. The heat of his own blood now running down his back was oddly comforting as he moved to straighten himself in the chair.

Riggs stepped back, rubbing his fist as Parr came back around the front.

'How ya know Long, pussyhole?' he yelled, pressing the broken blade into the soft skin below Jam's eye. Jam stared back defiantly.

'And what were you doing in Chatham?' Riggs chimed in.

Jam continued to stare ahead intently, but behind his eyes, his mind was focused on a plan. With both men now directly in front of him, he could reach behind with his right hand without being seen. The knife that Siobhan had handed him earlier was still concealed in his belt beneath Pete Jennings' jumper. He'd been so incapacitated by the blade in his shoulder that when they'd dragged him inside, they hadn't searched him, and the loose sleeves of the jacket were the only constraint around his hands. But now, as Riggs spoke, Jam saw that he was peeling gaffer tape from a roll and he knew he would only get one chance. He focused on Colin's eyes to prevent the pain showing on his face as he slowly lifted the hem of the jumper and grasped the handle.

***

Once more, he'd been ordered to rescue the sassy bastard who had punched him. This time, Mac got as close as the front door before something made him stop dead in his tracks. The car screeching to a halt, right in front of the house, was enough to make him dive for cover. But when he saw the man who got out, he knew he had to leave.

He'd seen that pig once before. The last time, years ago, he'd been able to get away unseen. Could he be that lucky again?

This was too much like history repeating itself. He waited in the shadows until the scum had gone past and then made his way out through the gate and down the street to the van. He drove away calmly; glad he could finally complete the task he'd started the evening before.

***

Parr had stepped back with the knife, and when Riggs limped around behind the chair, Jam was ready to attack. He knew the older man was the ruthless patriarch, but when it came to a fight, he needed to deal with the young thug first. It was also going to give him far more satisfaction to inflict first blood on the one man whose name had remained on his list for over a decade. Jam knew that if he could bury the knife deep enough into the flesh of Parr's thigh, it was likely to take him out of the fight at least long enough for him to deal with Riggs.

Riggs reached for Jam's left hand first, hoping to leverage the damage to his shoulder and stop him. Luckily for Jam, that meant he didn't even see the arc made by his right hand as he swung the blade around towards Parr's leg. Jam allowed the momentum of his swing to carry his whole body downwards so that the blade sliced as much as it stabbed with the full force of his weight. To stop his hand sliding along the blade, he locked his thumb rigid behind the end of the handle as the knife pierced the soft tissue of Parr's inner right thigh.

Parr went instantly to ground in a scream of outrage but his anger was quickly replaced with horror as the full impact of the knife deep in his leg hit home. Blood pulsed from the wound and he screamed as he reached forward for the handle until his eyes became glazed and his head fell backwards to the ground.

Jam's shoulder erupted with the pain of the movement as the sleeve took his arm with it away from Riggs' grip, until the jacket pulled itself inside out and freed his left hand. Fresh blood started to ooze from the wound, but it was a sacrifice Jam was happy to make, as he staggered up from the chair.

Riggs had lost his footing as easily as he had relinquished his grip on Jam's arm and he struggled to stay on his feet. With Jam satisfied there was no fight left in Parr, he turned to face the older man. Riggs stepped back; now without any of his thugs around him and no weapons to wield, he was a spent force, and he put his hands up in a brief moment of surrender. And then a smile broke on his lips. He was now looking beyond Jam, over his shoulder towards the door.

When Jam spun around, Natalie Riggs' hands were shaking but the gun was pointing square at his chest. At point blank range, she couldn't miss.

'Don't do it, Nat.' The voice came from the other door, behind Jam, and they all turned to see who it was. Jam didn't know him but the other two clearly did as the woman lowered her hands and dropped the gun.

'Tel,' Riggs said. 'We caught this intruder. He's already laid out Tommy. He's in the other room, not doing well. Carl doesn't look good either and... God knows where George is. I'm just defending my property. And protecting my family.'

'Alright, Ray. Calm down. Let's get some medics here and I'll sort this out.' He held out his warrant card to Jam and walked towards him. 'I'm DI Pinner and I'm arresting you on suspicion of kidnap, trespass and causing grievous bodily harm... and, most likely, attempted murder. You do not have to say anything...'

When Melville walked up the driveway to the house, Pinner was guiding Jam out through the door in handcuffs.

'Get some ambulances here, Jim. This one's left a trail of casualties. Three men down, two look serious. The other one will be breathing through a tube for a few weeks. And *he's* going to need treatment too – not that he deserves any.'

'Really,' Melville responded. 'I came back to rescue him.'

'What made you think that?'

'The girl.'

'You found her then. And you believe her?'

'But I thought the reason I came here was to help her.'

'Who said that, Constable?'

'Well... I thought *you* did, sir.'

'All I said was there was a woman acting strangely. It looks like she was in with this one all along. And he's like a one-man army, who's just wiped out half this household.'

'But sir, she was rescued from that house and had her trousers sliced open and her leg cut.'

'By him, most likely,' Pinner said. 'Go in there and see what he's capable of. And besides, who did you say rescued her?'

'There was a man, sir... in a Mercedes.'

'Did you interview him?'

'No, sir.'

'Get a name?'

'No... sir.'

'Well, Melville, these people tell a very different story. And I think I'd be inclined to believe the Chief Constable's neighbours, wouldn't you?'

'Ah... I see your point, sir. But...'

'Melville, you'd better take this one in. I'm happy for you to get the credit for sorting this mess out. It can't do you any harm when it comes to that transfer request.'

'Right... yes, sir. Thank you, sir.'

'And, Jim...'

'Yes, sir.'

'Now would be a good time to call this in, yeah?'

'I already have, sir.'

15.

Friday

Jam hoisted himself up with his right elbow as best as he could. The pillows kept sliding down on the slippery hospital mattress and he needed to try to keep weight off his left side. The X-ray that he'd had on arrival had shown up a triangle of metal lodged in his shoulder blade, and it hadn't been long before he was prepped for surgery. The painkillers were now doing their job and apart from not being able to sleep with worry for Siobhan, he was finally beginning to feel a little more comfortable. Of course, the handcuffs that secured his right wrist to the bedframe didn't help, but he felt sure the misunderstanding would be resolved and the police would start taking much more interest in Ray Riggs and his gang of thugs and kidnappers.

When the door to his individual ward opened, the copper who had sat and watched him sleep for the past few hours looked up. When he saw the detective constable walk in, he stood and left the room.

'Mr Michaels,' Melville said. 'How are you feeling?'

'You arrest any uvvers, man?'

'Er… we are still making enquiries about the events of last night. But, no… no other arrests.'

'You know dey kidnap da girl an' hold her in dat house? An' tie her up an' abuse her, yeah? Dat still a crime in dis country?'

'I've just been back to see Ms Jennings and I asked if she wanted to make a statement… about being abducted or mistreated… as may have appeared to have been the case last evening.'

'*Appear*? Wha'jer mean, man?'

'... and she has declined to press any charges against any of the men... that you attacked.'

'Uh-uh. You givin' me jokes, right?'

'No, her father has advised her to drop all the allegations she made last night and he has asked us to leave the matter at that.'

'Yer chattin' fraff, man. Let me phone her,' he said, shaking his head.

'I'm sorry, but they... or rather he... also asked that you don't contact her and... given your history of violent behaviour that they are now aware of, he has requested his lawyers to initiate injunction proceedings against you so that you must also stay away from her.'

'Nah, man. Dat's liber'ies.'

'I'm sorry, but they don't wish to be involved any further in the matter.'

'But people got bus' up, for real... I try to help her.'

'The people who got hurt badly... at least the ones who have regained consciousness; they *do* still wish to press charges... against you. Apart from the man in a coma, who happens to be the son of the owner of the property, another man almost bled out before he got here, but after about six pints of blood, you should be grateful he's still clinging to life. And a third man has serious facial injuries that will require extensive reconstructive surgery.'

'So wha'bout me, man? Wha'bout ma own injury? Dey not serious enough for you? What if *I* wanna press charges?'

'You were on *their* property... and you had a weapon.'

'It deir knife, man. Siobhan give it me when I rescue her.'

'As I was saying, they have a reasonable claim of self-defence against an intruder who had already caused grievous injuries to two of their staff.'

'Dat what dey call dem... staff? Dat's jokes. Dey clowns, man. For real.'

'From where I'm standing, that's entirely a matter of perspective.'

'Wha'bout ma facial injury in Cha'ham, man? An' wha'bout Jabba? He's da real victim. You know dat.'

'You signed a statement yesterday, saying that he had an accident, and you told me you had a fight in a pub. Are you now saying those were lies?'

''S'complica'ed, yeah. We was stitch up.'

'It's just a shame you couldn't have told me the truth yesterday. All of this might have been avoided.'

'I fought I could make it right.'

'So your actions last night were acts of revenge, is that what you're saying?'

'I'm sayin' nuffink, man.'

'That's probably the most sensible thing you've said since I walked in.' He sighed and looked around the room. 'Once you've been discharged by the surgeon, you will be taken into custody at Ilford police station and held there, pending further investigation. But, make no mistake, you should be prepared to be charged with a number of serious offences.'

16.

Nine weeks later

Raymond Riggs half-filled two crystal tumblers with Aberlour 25 and handed one to Detective Inspector Terence Pinner.

'Long time, no see, Tel.'

'How's your boy, Ray?'

'Looking good. All thanks to you. They say he should make a full recovery. Talking of boys... that Simon of yours must be growing up fast.'

'He's doing okay. Starting to come out of himself a bit more... The girl helps.'

'I'm glad to hear it, Tel.' Riggs nodded. 'She must be seventeen.'

'Out to work, now... apprenticeship. Turning out well. Got her wits about her. I think she'll go far.'

'Good to hear. No regrets then?'

'No. No regrets.' Pinner held up his drink, savouring the vapour before sipping the scotch.

'I'll drink to that,' Riggs said, and drained his glass. He shuffled across the room, fell back into his chair and pointed to another. 'Sit down, Tel. Time I started looking out for you a bit more... after what happened. I've been thinking, it's a good job you saw that lad hanging around outside when you left earlier that evening.'

'In this job, Ray,' Pinner said, leaning back into the leather upholstery, 'you get a nose for it. I could tell something was wrong. Lucky I knew one of the local boys... got him to take a look on the quiet.'

'Well, thanks. I owe you one.'

'Don't mention it. What about George, how's he doing?'

'You can ask him yourself, later. Always was an ugly bastard. I said to him, if anything, it's an improvement.'

Both men laughed.

'What about his wife? I heard there's still more they can do for her.'

'Not out of the woods, by a long shot. Poor bastard. Millstone round his neck from where I'm standing. Considering all the money he's throwing at her treatment.' Riggs smirked. 'As long as it's not our money, eh, Tel?'

'Yeah.' Pinner managed a half-hearted grin before his voice dropped. 'How did Monday go?'

'Oh, you know... never very pleasant. Nice service though... for Croydon. Didn't think they even had crematoriums down there in the wilds.'

'Yeah down south,' Pinner said, laughing, 'we tend to just leave them in the streets and let the wild dogs take 'em in the night.'

'Thought you might have shown your face, Tel.' The humour had dropped from Riggs' face like a dead man's chin. 'Would have meant a lot to Carl's mother.'

'You know I couldn't, Ray. I've had to keep my head down the last few weeks. Apart from a few awkward questions about what I was even doing around here, that local Met Constable has now joined my unit, so I've been showing him the ropes. He did good that night. I reckon he could be really useful.'

'So what can I do for you today, Tel? You name it.'

'No, I'm not looking for a favour... not today anyway. I just wanted to ask about that gear in your lock-up. That could get very hot, Ray. And like I said back then, I can't help you if that gets out.'

'You don't need to worry about that, Tel. I've told George, now he's back in action, he needs to get rid of it all.'

'What's the plan?'

'One night soon... out in the estuary. It'll take a few trips in the flat-bottom but he just needs to go out past low tide. There's

154

so much mud out there, no one will ever find it.'

'Tell him to take it easy. The current out there can be treacherous.'

'Yeah, well I might just go along with him... Make sure nothing goes wrong.' Riggs shook his head. 'And talking of silly bastards, what's happening about that crazy boxer?'

'Well, of course, he's facing a murder charge now. And he's got a whole load of history once we started digging. Group of Carl's mates came out of the woodwork. Even a couple of missing persons cold cases in the Croydon area over the last ten years are being reopened.'

'Don't forget about Ricky and Geordie, Tel. God knows what happened to them in the lock-up that day we first got Michaels and his sap.'

'He's denying any knowledge about what happened to them. He said he didn't kill them and they were still there when he left.'

'You'd think he'd come clean. It's not like things can get any worse for him.'

'Or he's protecting someone.'

'Has he coughed on Long yet?'

'Not a word.'

'He's got to be behind this. You said yourself there's a credible link between him and the house in Gravesend, where all that gear came from.'

'Yeah, we'll keep watching him.'

'And you know that was the place...' Riggs said, his features hardening, 'young Bobby was meant to go, the night he disappeared?'

Pinner nodded. 'Your brother. Yeah, I know.'

'Thirteen years last January. And your lot can't even come up with a theory for what happened to him.'

'We haven't given up, Ray,' Pinner said, nodding. 'One of these days, Long will make a big enough mistake and we'll bring him down.'

He hadn't told Riggs about the large quantity of blood that

Forensics now believed had been under the floor at the house where the goods had been seized. Without any DNA, there was no way of knowing whose blood it was, and it wouldn't help to give Riggs more reason to do something stupid to Long. Sometimes Pinner felt the best way to help Riggs was to protect the crazy sod from himself.

'Well, the day you do that, Tel...' Riggs was saying. 'That's the day you can retire, my old mate. I promise you, whatever you want, you can have... the day that piece of shit gets flushed away. Especially if it finally allows me to lay young Robert's memory to rest.'

When they shook hands, Riggs surprised Pinner with a large envelope that brought a smile to his face. As the policeman walked back to his car, he looked across to the neighbouring house owned by his Chief Constable and allowed himself a moment to imagine one day living next door to Raymond Riggs.

***

'Michaels, you've got a visitor.'

He followed the screw out of his cell and along the hall. The remand centre was modern and light but the smell of deviant, young men hung in the air.

Outside the relative calm of his room, he had to raise his defences. Everyone was looking for a weakness in everybody else. Something to exploit, someone to manipulate. Every inmate maintained a mantle of conceit to mask their fear. Behind the façade, they all hoped they could make it through to their day in court. Every outward appearance was false, every act intimidating. And everyone was innocent.

When the prison guard directed him into the casual visitor suite, he was expecting to find his lawyer sitting in one of the rooms. The man was middle-aged, with an air of superiority and a permanent frown. His visits were often out of the blue and he rarely seemed to have any news that gave Jam any confidence that he would receive a fair trial. His initial hopes for bail had been dashed at the first hurdle, and a month later, the case against him had suddenly become even more serious with Parr's death.

Yet that wasn't the worst of it. Some copper had subsequently reported seeing him at the lock-up the day after two other men had disappeared, and the CPS was now considering the possibility of adding their fate to his charge sheet, if and when their bodies were found.

It had now been seven weeks since that night, when things had gone so badly against him. He turned to go through the door and looked across the small room. Siobhan was sitting at the table, staring down at her hands. She stood up as he came in.

'Jam,' she said, 'I had to come.' She was about to walk around to him but the officer sitting in the corner held up his hand. By then, Jam had sat down anyway and without responding, continued staring into her eyes. 'Daddy wouldn't let me... before. But I've moved out. He can't stop me now. I've thought about you every day.'

'He got da right idea,' Jam said, expressionlessly. ''S'better you don't come. Leave it, Siobhan. It ain't wurf it... I ain't wurf it.'

'No, he's wrong. Just like he always is. Like he always *was*. I won't abandon you, Jam. Not like everyone else has.'

'Siobhan, dere's nuffink here for you. Ma brief say I could go down for twen'y years, man. We don't know each uvver. You can't give up your life like dat.'

She tried to maintain a look of hope in her eyes but he looked away. 'Jabba's doing well,' she said, and he turned back, the ghost of a smile crossing his face before it fell away.

'Dey even wanna blame me for him.'

'That's ridiculous, Jam. You would never hurt him. If only he could remember any of it... He told me to say hi. And as soon as he can, he'll come and see you.'

'Dat would be cool.'

She glanced at the guard who was looking out of the window and reached into her pocket

'I saw Herb,' she said in a whisper.

'Like he care.'

'He does,' she said, raising her eyebrows briefly as she put her hand flat on the table and slid it to the middle. He didn't move at first until her eyes darted to the guard and back to him. He reached across the table and stroked the soft skin with his fingers. When the guard coughed, she pulled her hand away slowly and left the piece of paper under his.

'I will stand by you, Jam,' she said. 'You did all that for me. And for him. We won't give up on you.'

Back in his room, he took the paper from his pocket, unfolded it and read the note.

> Jam, my friend, I'm sorry for how things have turned out. I did try to warn you but I couldn't have anticipated the connection with your past. That said, what happened was unacceptable. I can't turn the clock back and there is little I can do directly to help you now, but, if nothing else, this injustice will be avenged. And whatever happens, I will make sure that Jabba is well provided for and assist Siobhan any way I can in her commitment to support you.
>
> H

***

Harris eased the flat-bottom boat through the reeds and when it was held firm on the shore and concealed by the dark shadow of the warehouse, he walked back to the lock-up. Initially, he hadn't been keen on Riggs coming; surely he'd only be a liability with his gammy leg. But with Tommy still not allowed any exertion, Riggs had insisted, and Harris knew he would need help lifting the heavier pieces anyway.

Besides, he had already moved some of the parts he knew could still be shipped out to keep his customer happy until the next consignment arrived from Maracaibo. The profit on these two deliveries alone would cover Tracy's treatment in the States. He'd just have to be more careful next time. And he definitely wouldn't be including Riggs' son in any future side deals.

Riggs suggested they load all the smaller pieces into the trailer first and then helped him pull it through the gap in the fence behind the last row of garages and down to the water. Between them, they pushed the little boat out into the channel and Riggs held a tether line as Harris rowed about eighty yards into the estuary. When he was sure there were no other boats nearby, he dropped the metal parts over the side and rowed back, with Riggs pulling in the line.

It was slow and laborious work and they continued into the early hours. As they began lifting the heavier items, Harris really appreciated Riggs being there. Not only were there some pieces he couldn't have lifted into the trailer without help, but getting them over the side of the boat without it capsizing would have been impossible alone.

The last two trailer-loads had to be taken out in several trips. When Riggs looped up the rope, he clambered into the boat with Harris to help him lift it out again. They came back ashore for the last two pieces, which were so large they had barely been able to lift them into the trailer.

When they lowered the first one onto the deck, it sat heavily between the bench seats and, with the men standing either side, the boat was almost overrun as it sat so low in the water. They had no choice but to leave the last item for one final trip. It was a struggle to lift and push the thick steel disc over the side without going in with it, and on the way back in for the final piece, Riggs had to scoop out water as Harris rowed.

The last piece was a cylinder, almost two feet in diameter, with a thick rim welded to either end. They knew this was heavier than the last item and, nearing exhaustion, they could barely lift it over the edge of the boat. And when they stepped in and lowered it down, the displacement was almost too much. They sat down as smoothly and centrally as they could and as

Riggs pulled the rope in from the water behind him, Harris used an oar to push them slowly from the muddy bank. As he started to row, water came over the side with each stroke, but slowly they headed out into the channel. When they got as far out as they had before, Harris stopped rowing.

'A little bit further, George,' Riggs said.

'This is far enough.'

'It was further.'

'No, Ray,' Harris countered and pointed upstream. 'Look, those dredging markers line up. I've been using that as my guide. This is far enough.'

'But it's a bigger piece this time. We don't want it to get hooked up on the first boat that goes too close to the mud, do we, George?'

'No, but the current out in the middle will be too strong, if we go over, Ray. Are you sure that's wise?'

'It wouldn't hurt to go just a little further.'

'And risk killing us both?' he said, looking down at the water eddying around their feet.

'George, I'm not going to kill us both.' This time, when Riggs spoke, Harris recognised the tone. He'd heard it before. It was usually his wife Riggs spoke to in that way, when she'd annoyed him with some minor act of insolence or clumsiness. But he'd never used it on him before. Then, in the darkness, he saw the glint of metal in Riggs' hand and he froze.

'What's that? What are you doing? Ray, we're partners.'

'Keep rowing, George, nice and steady.' Riggs held the gun flat against his thigh, but Harris could see the silencer protruding beyond his kneecap and pointing straight at him. After three more strokes, the boat had drifted closer to the mid-channel when Riggs said, 'Right here, George. That's enough.' Harris put the oars down and the boat slowed. He hadn't realised that Riggs had untied the rope from the boat's cleat while they were still ashore and then pulled the loose end in when they set off. He now held out the entire length of rope looped in his hand.

'Take this,' he said, then pointed at the metal cylinder, 'and start threading it through the holes in the rim.'

'Ray,' Harris spluttered. 'I know I screwed up with this consignment, but it's all dealt with now. Look we drop this one and there's no harm done.'

'George, no one gets one over Raymond Riggs. And no one turns my own son against me. Pinner gave me the manifest and I had a little chat with Tommy about what you were both up to. I gave him a chance to make it up to me, given his condition. He went through the document and told me everything was there. I was even going to give you the benefit of the doubt, George. Put this down to a misunderstanding... of what was mine... and what was yours. Like you said, we're supposed to be partners. But, tell me, George, did we just clear the lock-up?'

'Yes, Ray.'

'Then where's the rest of it?'

'Ray, please... think about this. We can sort this out. Besides, if I go over, there's every chance you'll go with me. And with your leg, you won't get far in this current.'

'You don't think I thought about that, George?'

'You're bluffing. If I start rocking this boat, we'll both be done for.'

'You should always take precautions... when you're out on the water.' Riggs pulled back his coat to reveal the red low-profile vest. 'I doubt you thought about that, did you, George?'

'So you're going to float out to sea. Is that your big plan?'

'Stop worrying about me, George. Just start tying off that rope. Or... this far out, I doubt that anyone would hear a gunshot, anyway. At least this way, I'm giving you a chance, George... That's right, thread it through and now around your waist...'

'You see the other precaution I don't suppose you took...' he continued, 'was to tell someone... and I mean someone you could actually trust... tell them what you were doing tonight and where you'd be. No, of course you didn't. Well, I did. And he's watching us now in case anything goes wrong. Of course, he's not aware of this little twist, but I'm sure he can be persuaded to remain loyal when you have your little accident.'

'So, now what, Ray? Have you really thought this through? Were you really expecting me to help you lift that over the side?'

'You never could see all the angles, could you, George. The water's now up to our ankles. How much longer before this thing sinks?'

'You can't seriously think we're going to sit here until we sink? It'll be daylight before then.'

'What if I did this?' He took aim at the bottom of the boat and fired. 'What about now?' With the silencer, the gun hardly made a sound shooting through wood into the water, and after the third shot, the wood had shattered and water began pooling rapidly around their legs.

'Jesus!' Harris yelled. 'If you were gonna do that anyway, why didn't you just shoot me?'

'I want to give you time, George... time to think about what you've done.'

'But, Ray, please... I'm begging you. Think about Tracy. We're so close to a breakthrough. If you kill me, you'll be killing her too.'

'No George,' Riggs said. 'You don't put that on me. This is all on you,'

As water started gushing over the side, Riggs slid into the river, triggering the life vest to inflate under his coat. The boat disappeared beneath the surface. Harris took his last gulp, and before being pulled under, instead of the satisfaction of seeing his so-called partner drift downstream with the tide, he caught a glimpse of a length of cord breaking the surface, as someone began reeling Raymond Riggs into the shore like the big fish he always was.

EPILOGUE

Eight Years Later
September

He walked through the passage towards the kitchen. The heavy doors either side were locked; the strong rooms hadn't been used for years. Now he had a bigger place out in the country, he'd finally be letting this old house go. It had served its purpose, but there was one thing left to deal with. The dresser behind the door was thick with dust as he pulled open the drawer. He removed the object he'd discarded there at the turn of the new millennium and dropped it into his pocket.

As he turned to leave, he noticed the cupboard door beneath the sink was slightly open. There were some old rags wedged at the bottom, preventing it from closing. He reached down and opened the door, and the material fell onto the floor. He picked it up and held it to the window. The first thing he noticed as it unravelled were the dark stains dried into the pale blue fabric. He repositioned it in his hands and held the garment by the shoulders. It looked like a summer dress with its short sleeves. But the single breast pocket had letters embroidered on it. The smaller print beneath the logo had faded, but the three capitals were unmistakeable. NHS.

He tried to remember if there had ever been a nurse in this old house. He recalled the first time Siobhan came here to check on those injured lads, and there *had* been a lot of blood that night. But he knew it couldn't have been hers; she wasn't even qualified back then. In the intervening years, he had kept his word and supported her as she campaigned tirelessly in support of Jam's appeal. His sentence was subsequently reduced and she went back to finish her training to fill her time while she waited for him. Jabba remained on the payroll but all Herb ever asked of him was to occasionally help Mac with the heavy lifting.

That's when it struck him. The hairs on the back of his neck bristled. He remembered Siobhan's inspiration had been her mother, and now he recalled the tragic story of her disappearance. She had never been found. He closed his eyes and shook his head. Surely, now he had to act.

Turning to look at the pile of rubbish on the table, the idea that had been no more than a sentimental whim after his recent conversation with Annie started to come together in his head. He took a brown envelope and a sheet of newspaper from the assortment of junk mail. He wrapped the garment in the newssheet and swapped it for the object in his pocket. The small rectangular box went into the envelope, which he placed among the debris on the table and walked away.

THE END

If you loved Jammed Up, you might also enjoy

 When a debt goes bad...

...someone's looking to make a killing.

Michael Field just lost his City job and his beautiful wife in one fell swoop. Unemployed and down on his luck, he is propositioned by one-time friend, Herbert Long. The job is non-negotiable. It's pay-back for a cover-up years ago. But something's not right; it all seems too easy.

And it's not just the job that doesn't add up. Part of him is flattered by the improbable advances of the beautiful young woman who calls herself Grace de Manton, but his inner realist is suspicious. What is her game? Could she be connected with Herb somehow? He can't shake the feeling he's being watched. Then there's the voice of a stranger, threatening him down the phone... and that man lurking in the shadows.

In this complex criminal web, Mickey doesn't know who to protect and who to fear. But with even those closest to him seemingly involved, who can he trust? A hapless pawn in a bigger game that's playing out between local crime lords, all he knows is whatever happens, he's not going back into that bloody chamber!

Turn the page to sample the opening chapters.

AN EXTRACT FROM

MICKEY

TAKE

PROLOGUE

December 1983
Monday, 5th

Fog hangs in garlands from the sparse trees along an unlit road. The night is frozen, bone-deep. It's no longer silent. Neither is it holy. Branches weep from the shudder of impact. Screams of agony splinter the air. And hot metal pings. Two cars have recoiled, face off, astride white lines. Festooned with shards of silver and gold, the tarmac glistens like Christmas.

Minutes later, beyond the next bend, another motor stops abruptly. Seeing the blue flickering trees ahead, the driver's brain immediately spikes. He kills the engine and snuffs the headlights and, once out of the car, checks all the locks before disappearing into the shadows.

At the turn in the road, his first glimpse of the scene is the rear of a white hatchback. Viewed from behind, it appears unscathed, its street cred emblazoned in black letters across the tail. The other car facing him is crushed beyond recognition. Its red bonnet curls upwards like a tin lid. Ahead, at the foot of a tree, a heap of limbs and clothing lay deathly still. On seeing the traffic cop, the watcher instinctively drops to the ground. He breathes deeply as his knees soak up the muddy verge, until the piercing screech of metal clears his head.

Failing noisily to prise open its door, the cop speaks softly to the driver of the red car. With no more than a sideways glance at the woman on the ground, whose living eyes wouldn't stare that way, he hurries on, past the steaming bonnet of the hatchback, ignoring the gaping hole in its windscreen. The exchange with this driver is more animated; two deep voices with an edge of familiarity talk at length. Eventually, the cop crosses the road to check on the body.

The watcher remains concealed, aroused by the carnage.

It's a futile gesture when the plod holds his fingers to the woman's neck. Even the awkward rearranging of her coat to cover her exposed flesh is made to look dignified. But when he deliberately pulls on his gloves, lifts the limp calf and roughly removes her shoe, the unseen witness sneers.

He's seen it all before. Where were the bizzies when a fleeting uncle broke his arm in a drug-fuelled rage? Or when his ma smacked his head against the wall to back up the story of how the clumsy five year old had fallen downstairs? Where were they a few years later, when he was forced to beg for her on East End streets, so she could score her next fix? They just moved him along. And the one time he went to them and opened up, they ignored his cry for help.

Nothing surprises him now. Not when the pig walks back to the white car, opens the nearside door and drags the screaming driver across to the passenger seat. Nor when he goes back to the driver's door and hurls the woman's shoe into the foot well. Not even when he returns to the body, removes her blood-soaked scarf, wraps it around his baton and slams it through the shattered windscreen, widening the hole. When the silk snags on the broken glass, he leaves it hanging there like ribbon.

Only then does the scum return to his patrol car and call for paramedics. Only then, with all the justification he will ever need, does the watcher return to his car to await the blare of sirens that will cover his retreat. And only then does his mind return to the task of dumping the body parts bagged up in his boot.

1.

September 2009
Wednesday, 16th

No taller than five-four, she shoulders her way through the pack with the wiry strength of a fly-half. As a gap opens she falls forward, unsteady in three-inch heels, leaning against my arm with one hand, whilst deftly cradling two glasses in the other. I move awkwardly to make way, but rather than try to pass she smiles and says, 'I've been watching you.'

She asks my name; hers doesn't register. After the evening I've had, you wouldn't blame me. But I must look a complete imbecile when all I can say is, 'Uh?'

'Grace,' she repeats, and this time the adolescent in my head whispers, *Amazing*.

She really is. An innocent, heart-shaped beauty with big, docile eyes set deep into sculpted cheekbones, reminding me of those sultry caricatures, popular in the 60s. The only outward signs of the gregarious nerve that allows her to approach a complete stranger in a crowded bar are the upturned corners of her smile. The way they exaggerate the mischievous dimples at either side of her mouth only competes for my attention with the sparkle in her eyes.

'Macallan, isn't it?' she says, offering me one of the drinks. 'I prefer something a bit peatier, like a Lagavulin or Laphroaig, but this'll do for now.'

She downs the whisky with only a slight grimace, and continues to press the second glass into my hand, before looking at me with a fixed grin, probably wondering if there's anyone in. Hello? I pull my eyes away from hers, zooming out for a wider view. She's obviously not long out of the weather because her shoulder-length blonde hair hangs down in shaggy, damp twists like she just stepped out of the shower.

Okay, I'm going to hold that thought...

Hot Shot

My name is Michael Field. If you thought I was going to say: *My name is Michael Caine*, you'd be wrong. The only thing we've got in common, some say, is he talks like me. I suppose you'll be the judge of that. Anyway, call me Mickey.

I'm here in my local. About nine miles east of a place I've affectionately dubbed Bleak House. I've just covered twice that distance getting back. You've seen the movie with the guy, freaked out and running, flushed into the underground labyrinth. That was me. Going north on the Central line... over the loop to Hainault... above ground, through busy streets... another tube, heading south... first bus, going anywhere... District Line, eastbound... one beyond my usual stop... off at Hornchurch... walk a random circuit back... before slipping unnoticed into the sanctuary of a familiar watering hole...

After that, the first single malt wasn't likely to touch the sides. Was I followed by a thug wielding a torch? I don't think so. Did I see any psychos along the way? Well, it *was* London. But no, none of them were in hot pursuit, so I thought I was in the clear.

Unusually for a Wednesday, The Feathers was heaving when I squeezed my way to the bar, avoiding any eye contact. The barmaid was another new face out of the usual mould – chirpy, young Antipodean with a mercenary smile, razor-sharp wit and a mood that could turn on a sixpence. She was being chatted up by some lads along the bar and didn't given me a second glance as I twitched down the first glass and immediately called for another.

The second scotch had been sitting on the bar for a couple

of minutes. My heart had stopped pounding, and I was feeling confident I could pick up the glass without spilling any this time. As I did, a hand rested on my shoulder and I lurched forward with a jolt in horror at the thought of a guy with a Maglite grabbing my arm and hauling me from the pub. It was just some reveller getting carried away and tripping towards the bar. I called him an arsehole under my breath while licking whisky off my hand. I could tell he was too drunk to notice me and too arrogant to give a shit. He was wearing a dark suit and fancy cuffs, just like I used to. The Feathers is always full of drunken City tossers on an England match night. They slowly regress into unlikely hooligans – voices become more raucous, language more colourful – as they direct all that suppressed male aggression at the big screen.

Having shifted position to let him in, I feigned nonchalance and cast my eyes around the pub. The bar in The Feathers is like a big horseshoe, with an island in the middle that the staff can circle around. Evenly spaced around it are elaborately-carved pillars, supporting glass shelves above, framing my view through to the other side. That's when I saw her, an absolute babe, leaning against the bar directly opposite and staring straight back at me.

Without a TV screen, that side of the pub didn't seem so busy, and I thought she might have been on her own. On one side of her was a space that was soon taken by an old guy, waving a fiver vigorously towards the landlord who was covering that part of the bar preferred by his football-indifferent regulars. On the other side was a middle-aged couple in conversation, their backs to my apparent admirer. She was being served. The landlord put down two tumblers. I was relieved, though slightly disappointed, because that surely meant her boyfriend was at one of the far tables. I looked away, mildly bemused by the intensity of the moment.

I tried to keep my cool but I could still feel her eyes on the back of my head. I had to look back. By then the barmaid was standing right in front of me, setting down two pints of lager for

City Boy. When she moved back to the Guinness pump to fill the final third of a glass, my view across the pub returned and I was looking at a gap at the bar next to the old guy talking to the landlord. Game over. I downed the second scotch without a further spillage and contemplated taking the back roads home.

While the last couple of hours had felt like a nightmare, I knew I wasn't dreaming. But what occurred next surely only happened to guys like me in a fantasy world of our own making, in the depths of a beer-induced coma. I turned to make my exit and thought about nudging The Suit's drinking arm as I pushed my way to the door, when the gap I was trying to open up was suddenly blocked by the girl from across the bar, squeezing her way towards me.

Alarm bells started ringing in my head and this evening's main event flashed through my mind...

Bleak House

When you fall on hard times, there's no knowing how low you'll stoop. But believe me, I wasn't doing it for fun. And although I knew what I was looking for, I didn't really understand why it was so important to Herb, nor why it was worth the four figures he was paying me for this little bit of breaking and entering.

The thought crossed my mind: if the place looked like it had been deserted for years, was it still technically a crime to break in? Either way, it wasn't like it was the first I'd ever committed. It might have been fair to say that everyone had done the odd ton down the motorway or had a few too many sherbets and didn't want to leave the car at the station overnight. But that's not what I was thinking. My previous experience was somewhat more serious than antisocial behaviour behind the wheel. That was a long time ago, and then I had some help when it came to tidying up the loose ends. Suffice to say, nothing ever came of it and I was able to get on with my life.

I'd always fancied myself as a lucky boy, a charmer, what they used to call a Likely Lad. Even so, I couldn't help feeling there was something very iffy about this job. I was about to commit only my second attempt at burglary and, much like twenty years ago, I didn't really know what I was letting myself in for.

Undeterred, I slid effortlessly through an open sash window onto a squalid, threadbare carpet. At one time it might have had a swirling pattern, but more of its mesh backing was showing than any of the abstract scrolls of its former glory. It wasn't quite as dark in this room as it had been out the back. While a single streetlight shone in from the front, my eyes still found it hard to adjust. Outside, its intrusive glare had been subdued by the irregular shadow of a large oak that conveniently obscured the side path from the road, allowing me a discreet way around from the garden.

If I said the light was casting an amber wash around the room, glowing and fading rhythmically like a mood lamp as the tree swayed gently in the breeze, I'd be having you on because I was completely unmoved by the ambience of the place. If I went on to say the sepia hue made the room seem welcoming and benign, you'd know I'd lost the plot. But I did sense a strange contradiction in the apparent tranquillity. That feeling I'd had – that something wasn't right about this, not just morally and legally – it hadn't gone away. This was too easy. The window on the side of the house hadn't even been latched for Christ's sake; not exactly breaking and entering when all I had to do was lift the bloody window and step in. I couldn't believe my luck. Although once I was in and looking around that dingy little room, any optimism I had, soon began to dampen.

I couldn't make out the colour of the floor or the fringed, partly-shredded bedspread, thrown untidily across the single bed that ran the entire length of the wall. The bed was basic, reminding me of a prison bunk: metal-framed, no headboard, a thin striped mattress, visible where the cover didn't obscure it, no pillow, or any other sign of comfort. Apart from that, a frayed wicker chair in the corner by the window and an ancient wardrobe opposite, the room was empty. It was the wardrobe that held my attention, one of its doors gaped and the remains of an inner mirror were strewn in flickering shards across the floor.

Tiny slivers of glass crackled underfoot and the carpet clung to my shoes like Velcro as I stepped out into the hallway. To my right, I could only just see the bottom step of a staircase that ascended off to the side. I shuddered, barely suppressing the memory of a stranger looking down at me from the landing. That was another staircase, in another house, long ago. Beyond this one was the front door, its rippled glass glimmering orange from the neon outside. Across the hall were two more rooms. The door to the front room was shut. The other was open, and I could see a linoleum floor, streaked with what looked like oil.

The floorboards creaked in protest as I took a step towards the open door. The edge of a rolled-top bath, the kind that would cost a fortune to buy, came into view. Above, I could only discern the outline of a small frosted window, presumably facing out onto the wall of the neighbouring house, because it added no illumination to the room. Without opening the door wider, I could only see one side of the bath; its once pristine white enamel looked grey and dull, seemingly smeared with the same greasy muck as the floor.

I tried to ignore the flashback in my head, reminding me what pools of blood looked like in the dark. Too late. What little I could see was already combining with vivid memories. My confidence was ebbing away on a wave of revulsion at the disgusting state of this place. Nausea was creeping up on me as the smell registered with my senses. A dank, suffocating odour of decay permeated the walls and rose from the floor in an acrid vapour; a stomach-churning cocktail of stagnant piss, sour milk and vomit.

And there was something else: a sweet, pungent edge with the tang of rotting meat and the bitterness of cold metal.

Moments before, easing through the window, my mood was bright. This was easy. No problem. Grab it and go. Now I felt sick. What the hell had I walked into? I was frozen, in the middle of the hallway, unable to move.

What possessed you to get involved in something Herb's tied up with? The voice of Michael the Banker echoed in my head.

— Stick with it. Into the kitchen, two more paces and you're there. You know where it is. Get in there, pick it up and leg it back out through that window.

Mickey the Resurgent Rebel won the debate and I was moving again.

Old instincts took over and I strode headlong towards the door at the end of the hall. Like the bathroom, the door was ajar and beyond it there was only darkness. I knew, once in the kitchen, I'd be able to get my bearings and locate what I came for. I slowly pushed the door, letting in light from the hall, and stepped over the threshold. I stopped abruptly, confused and disoriented. What I was looking at wasn't the kitchen.

It was a connecting room, wider than the hall, no more than ten feet long. I had to assume it led in turn to the kitchen. I tried to make sense of the unexpected layout, comparing it in my mind to the outer perimeter I'd had to skirt around. That's when I realised there were two other rooms, one on either side of me, and I was merely standing in another rectangular hallway, this one with a door on each of its four walls. The one ahead had to be the kitchen and it was partially open, whereas the solid doors on either side were both closed.

As I looked from one to the other it was apparent that although the rest of the house hadn't been maintained for donkey's years, these internal walls had been added in more recent times. Left un-plastered in bare cinder block, their dull grey doors were set into unfinished metal frames, each with robust bolts top and bottom – the ones on the door to my right were secured by heavy duty combination locks. The concrete floor, also not an original feature, was levelled only to a rough screed.

In any other circumstance I'd have been intrigued by the industrial nature of the renovation, in what was otherwise an uninhabitable dump, but my head was spinning with the reek that intensified as I got deeper into the building. It was like I'd entered a huge corpse and was being drawn towards its putrefying guts. The smell assaulted my senses, adding to a surging feeling of dread at what surrounded me. I tried to stay focused as I pulled up my collar to cover my nose and mouth and walked straight ahead, into the kitchen.

Scanning the mountain of rubbish on the table, it didn't take me long to see it. There, wrapped in an oversized brown envelope, a package no bigger than a paperback. I could tell before I even looked inside, it was the object I'd come for, and I put it in my pocket. It was so light I knew I'd need to keep checking it was still there. A feeling of satisfaction lifted me and I headed back with renewed confidence, reaching the doorway into the original hall, ready to get the hell out of there. That's when I took leave of my senses.

— Hey, what's the rush? It's cool. I've got what I came for, no problem. This is easy. I got in quick. I can get out quicker. No one's seen me, there's no one around. Let's take a quick look at this added room – the one with the bolts drawn back. Maybe there's something else in there that would be useful to Herb.

Ever the opportunist, the Resurgent Rebel took control and, with a newfound enthusiasm, I was heading back to investigate the chamber.

The handle turned readily, and I pushed. The door yielded quietly, smooth yet heavy on sturdy hinges, inward into total blackness. Although there were no windows, it wasn't the darkness I noticed first. Released from its confined space, the stench hit me like a train and made me gag. Reeling at the thought of grisly scenes that might have played out in this hellish cell, I retched, almost adding to the assumed matter on the floor.

Somehow I mustered the mental and physical gristle to step into the room, and my eyes began to adjust to what tentative light had dared follow me in. All I could see was a metal bench, scattered with an assortment of tools: lump hammer, pliers and a hacksaw. Don't be fooled, this was no DIY workshop. The meat cleaver and various butchers' knives and skewers removed any lingering doubt, as clinically as they would any other surplus appendage. I'd seen enough and was ready to leave when I spotted something else on the bench. It was another brown envelope, at first sight, much like the one nestling in my pocket. That was just another trick of the light. No, this one was like a brick, a solid wad, constricted by rubber bands, stretched taut around its length and width into a thick, twisted cross.

I was drawn to it. Maybe I was thinking it would make a good counterweight in my jacket, like ballast for the voyage home. *Yeah right.* Maybe I wasn't thinking at all because even before I put it in the other pocket, I knew it would tip the scales *so* far the other way.

Pulling the door behind me was surprisingly easy and it picked up its own momentum and slammed with a reverberating clang. While it gave me some reassurance the door would keep whatever evil had occurred there contained, it also shattered the stillness of the house and echoed noisily as I retreated to the main hallway.

No sooner had I turned to enter the bedroom on the right, I heard another sound – a hideous, muffled scream – a human cry so desperate and pathetic that it reached through my chest and tore at my lungs. I froze again, not knowing what to do. I was convinced the voice had come from the locked room. The last thing I wanted to do was go back in there.

I didn't get far before a loud rattling sound shrink-wrapped my testicles. It was the front door, ten feet behind me. Someone else was trying to get into the house. Okay, call me a coward, but if I said something like this had happened before, you'd forgive me the perverse sense of relief as I abandoned all thoughts of chivalry. Besides, this was way too much aggro for the sake of a thousand quid, and my instinct to flee was stronger than any human urge to stay and help whoever might be suffering in that room. I was through the bedroom and out of the window quicker than I came in, moving silently and swiftly back down the garden, towards the high fence along the back.

I glanced over my shoulder, expecting some knucklehead

to be pursuing me, the open window of my escape surely obvious to anyone coming into the hall. I was relieved to see no one chasing. It was only when I'd clambered up, and was about to drop down the other side of the fence, that I got a good look back at the house and saw the torch illuminating the kitchen like a strobe, while a ghostly silhouette ransacked the room.

Before I lowered myself to safety, the shadow of a giant appeared at the window and the searchlight's beam swept across my face.

Bunny Girl

Since escaping down the gravel pathway that runs along the backs of the gardens of Bleak Neighbourhood, I'd been replaying the scene in my mind. Between anxiously looking about to see if I was being followed, and frantically scouring the tube map I'd pulled from one of the station racks en route, I wasn't able to get the thought from my head that someone had been suffering in that place and I'd just run away.

Now here I am, being chatted up by the most beautiful, young woman I've ever seen.

Maybe she's the girlfriend of the guy with the torch. It's The Banker again, trying to cramp my style. Maybe she's going to soften you up and lure you into a dark alley where he'll be waiting with his toolkit.

— No. That's just being paranoid.

Maybe she's a prostitute?

— She doesn't look like one.

Like you'd know what they look like.

— Yeah, I'm pretty sure they don't go around buying their prospective clients drinks as if they're selling time-shares. Even tarts have standards.

Fair point.

I'm confused. Amidst the conversation in my head, my brain can't find the right connections to work out what to do. It's trying to recall the last time a gorgeous girl with a taste for single malt introduced herself with a sexy smile and a free drink.

When I was a young guy – ready, willing and able – this never happened to me. In twelve years of marriage, this never happened to me. Yet here I am, well past my prime, down on my luck, in an old Barbour coat that hangs down on one side, and looking like I've spent the evening with Freddy Krueger. And completely out of the blue, I'm supposed to know what to say.

'Thanks' is the best I can manage. God, I'm so pathetic. I need to get a grip soon before she comes to the conclusion that I have some kind of mental impairment and a nightly visit to the pub is part of my care in the community programme. All I can do is raise the drink and sip it like a girl.

Fortunately, the kick of the spirit jolts my brain from its inertia and I look around for somewhere we can sit or at least have some space to move. There's a small table in the corner and I nod in its direction.

'Sorry,' I say as she sits down with her back to the window. 'You must think I'm a complete moron. It's just that... you caught me a bit cold. Hello, I'm Mickey.'

'I did start to worry I'd made my biggest chat-up mistake ever,' she teases, 'but I'm always ready for rejection.'

I smile at the Betty Boop tilt of her head that confirms my belief she's never had to worry about that.

'So, Mickey... were you heading off already?'

Her eyes seem to shine into mine, like she's driving towards me around a sharp bend, intentionally leaving them on full beam. I'm blinded, mesmerised, imminent road-kill, unable to avoid staring back into them. I try to retain some composure and take control, but I'm hopelessly outwitted at every turn.

'Oh, I only popped in for a quick one,' I reply, instantly aware of the clumsy innuendo. My obvious discomfort is met with a naughty smile that lights up her face.

'I'm sure I counted two,' she says, lowering her gaze from my eyes. 'You're obviously a guy who doesn't hang around.'

Unlike mine, her double-entendre is both subtle and intentional, and I feel my face flush and my pulse quicken. I grin like a schoolboy and shift awkwardly in the chair.

For God's sake get a grip; you're probably old enough to be her father.

I try to assume some semblance of seniority by finishing the rest of the scotch and asking her if she'd like another drink.

'This time, I'll get them to add some peat,' I joke embarrassingly as I turn to go to the bar.

'Okay,' she calls after me. 'But if Pete's not around, I'll settle for Mickey.'

Now, as I walk to the bar, everything is different. City Boy moves aside to let me through and I'm served without waiting by the Aussie barmaid who smiles sweetly and even says 'Thanks, mate,' when I hand her a tenner. It's turning into one very interesting night, and already I've completely forgotten about the odd packages in my coat pockets and the anguished cry for help that turned my legs to jelly less than two hours ago.

Grace brings me back to reality with a bang when she asks what I've been up to this evening. She admits she's been watching me from the other side of the bar and thought I looked seriously worried about something. Where do I start? Those big eyes are hard to deceive, and I have to keep looking away as I come up with some cock and bull story about Mum being ill. She seems to fall for it and gives me lots of sympathy. She says she spent the evening helping her brother with his homework. I think I got away with my little white lie about poor mother's gout, but they say it takes a bull-shitter to know one, and I'm having serious doubts that Grace is being completely straight with me.

For some reason I can't fathom, the conversation seems to be getting tense. I suspect I'm reacting subconsciously to her apparent change of mood. She's trying too hard to make meaningless conversation and I'm wondering if things aren't moving a bit too quickly for someone I've only just met. The grown-up in me takes back control and I start looking for a way to bring this interesting and very flattering fantasy to a close, at least for the time being. Apart from anything else, I'm getting really anxious to call Herb.

The rabbit in the headlights analogy begins to take on a more sinister meaning as I sense Grace realising the evening's conquest is coming to a premature end. The bunny's in serious danger of being boiled and the cheeky banter is turning into sarcasm and resentment.

'Well you'd better head off home if you've got a better offer waiting there,' she says after I start making noises about needing to get an early night with a busy day ahead.

I want to see her again, I really do, but all I can come up with when I get up to leave is, 'I'm sure I'll see you in here again sometime.'

'Probably not the best offer I'm going to get tonight,' she replies brutally.

Harsh... but fair. The Banker gets the last word as I squeeze my way to the door.

***

Another Mother

The soothing sound of violins drifts along the hall to the room he's checking first. The music adds to his relief at finding the door untouched. He's been caught off-guard – came back to clean up too late. It's much earlier in the evening than he'd expected, though it's not for him to reason why. Ask no questions; tell no lies. Do as he's told... most of the time. As for the rest... he's only trying to help. That's what's concerning him now. The fact it's all still here. That wasn't in The Plan. Opening the door, he exhales loudly. Everything's as he left it. But that other room... that's another matter.

Lighting it up, his first concern is addressed; still there, in a bucket, behind the door. He'll get rid of it later. That's two off his list – the worst half. The other two, they're not bad things. Not really. But they are of more value... at least to him. He looks around and his jaw tightens at the sight of an empty space where he'd left the first. Ought to be more careful...

'How many times do I have to tell you not to leave your shit lying around?' He hears her voice and freezes. 'How... many... times...?' Each word accompanied by the sting of her hand.

How many times? How many times had he gone to his bed hungry... to grip with little fingers the red imprint swelling his thin, freckled arm... to feel the comforting warmth soak through his scants... to spend the night praying to be dry by morning...

Seeing the other thing still there brings him back. His face softens and he relaxes his fist. Crossing the room, he smiles and, lifting it gently, wipes the glass with his sleeve. She smiles back and he takes it with him, his steps lighter as he cradles it in time with the music.

Mickey Take: When a debt goes bad... is available to purchase in paperback and kindle editions on Amazon. Signed and personalised copies of the paperback can be purchased for UK delivery, direct from the author's web-site:

http://www.stevenhaywardauthor.com/#buy-direct

ABOUT THE AUTHOR

After a happy childhood, growing up on the Hamworthy peninsula of the beautiful Poole Harbour in the county of Dorset, Steven progressed from the local grammar school to an international bank, then based in Poole, with the promise of travel and high finance. Alas, it was to be another fourteen years before he would make his first overseas business trip... to Jersey in the Channel Islands! But in the years that followed, working for several City institutions, he travelled far and wide managing relationships with large institutional clients, before settling into the compliance role of Money Laundering Reporting Officer. In recent years he has divided his time between his love of writing and consulting on financial crime. He lives in Kent with his wife and their beagle Ella.

THE LAST WORD

Readers' reviews are vitally important to all authors, but especially to the self-published ones like me, without the backing and marketing muscle of a large publishing house behind us. If you enjoyed reading Jammed Up: a Debt Goes Bad novella, please leave a review on your local Amazon site and on Goodreads.com if you are a member. It would really mean a great deal to me.

Thank you,
Steven Hayward
May 2016

Please visit my web-site and sign up for news and information on upcoming releases. Subscribers can also download the e-book edition of Jammed Up absolutely free:

> http://www.stevenhaywardauthor.com

Join me on Facebook:

> https://www.facebook.com/StevenHaywardAuthor

Follow me on Twitter:

> https://www.twitter.com/stevieboyh

www.ingramcontent.com/pod-product-compliance
Lightning Source LLC
Chambersburg PA
CBHW030251130626
46549CB00002B/477